S.P.I.R.I.T.S.

of New England®
HAUNTINGS, GHOSTS & DEMONS
A Collection of Short Stories
By

Accomplished Paranormal Investigator & Author
Jack Kenna

Cover Art and Inside Art Illustrated By
Alex Cormack

All photos provided by S.P.I.R.I.T.S. of New England®
and the Author Jack Kenna

ISBN: 154482162X
ISBN-13: 978-1544821627

Library of Congress Control Number: 2017908894
CreateSpace Independent Publishing Platform, North Charleston, SC

ABOUT THE AUTHOR

Paranormal Investigator, Technical Specialist, Author, Public Figure, Husband, Father, Grandfather, and member of the paranormal teams S.P.I.R.I.T.S. of New England®, San Diego Ghost Hunters®, Extreme Paranormal Encounter Response Team, and honorary member of Wraith Paranormal Research Society of North Carolina. Jack is also a Senior Engineering Technician for the Department of the Army. He is a regular contributor to Paranormal Underground Magazine and Living Paranormal Magazine. In 2015 he created and authored the comic *S.P.I.R.I.T.S. – The Forgotten Souls of Bay Path* which was illustrated for him by Alex Cormack, the original story of which now appears in this book. Jack has also appeared in numerous episodes of the television series Paranormal Survivor, and is a series lead on Haunted Case Files, both shows air on cable network Destination America in the USA, and the Travel & Escape (T&E) network in Canada. The shows also air in the UK and Europe. Jack will be releasing a new non-fiction book about investigating the paranormal in the spring of 2018 through Schiffer Publishing, Ltd.

DEDICATION

This book is dedicated to my children Joshua, John, Elora, Olivia, Joseph, Johnnie, and Marena. Always do what is right and not what is easy, have goals, aspire to them, work hard, do not let anyone stand in your way, and have FAITH.

Disney World 2009

FAITH IS STRENGTH

CONTENTS

"Choose your path based on your passion and your gifts, be determined, be kind, be honest, work hard, have faith, believe, and you will succeed."

~ Jack Kenna ~

ACKNOWLEDGMENTS

I would like to thank my S.P.I.R.I.T.S. of New England team and extended family; Founders Ellen MacNeil and Beck Gann, Co-Founders Sharon Koogler and Sarah Campbell; thank you all for allowing me to be part of this wonderful and somewhat dysfunctional little family. We have been through a lot together and weathered it all, we have come such a long way in a short time and made many friends along the way, as well as lost a few. We have helped many, many people and we will help many more, because that is what investigating the paranormal is about for us. Thank you for letting me tag along on this great journey with all of you. A special thank you to my friend Katie Boyd, who inspired me to pursue my passion for writing and the paranormal, and to my friend Beckah Boyd who has guided me wisely on my own personal journey into the spiritual side of the paranormal. You have shown me that I should not fear the abilities I have just because I do not understand them, and that I should embrace them, and to use them to bring comfort and understanding to those who are in need.

Blessed Be.

INTRODUCTION
WHAT'S IN A NAME

While this book is a work of fiction; well at least for the most part it is, but I will not tell you which parts; I did want to take a moment to reflect on my team S.P.I.R.I.T.S. of New England® and a little bit of its' history.

S.P.I.R.I.T.S. as it has come to be known, was founded on 10 January 2009 by Ellen MacNeil, Beck Gann, Sharon Koogler, and Ellen's daughter Sarah Campbell. In spite of some popular belief I, Jack Kenna, am not the founder of the team, nor was I an original member. I was graciously asked to join the team sometime later after meeting all of them at a paranormal event at the Spalding Inn in New Hampshire. I was not made a full-fledged member until December of 2009. Once a member of the team I thought about how cool it was to be part of a paranormal team called S.P.I.R.I.T.S.! Although as someone once told me, it is not the name, but what you make it stand for that matters. You see, back in those early years after the famous television shows started to air, everyone wanted to create a paranormal team, and having a cool name seemed to be the most important thing to start with. Then came the black shirts and the cool logo because hey, you were not a real paranormal team without those things…right? In the end though many of those teams went by the way side because they missed the real point. It was not about what the name meant or how cool it looked on a logo, what mattered was what the name stood for.

Now the individual letters of S.P.I.R.I.T.S. in *S.P.I.R.I.T.S. of New England* stand for Supernatural, Paranormal, Investigations, Research, Intuitive, Truth, Society. The real question though is what does S.P.I.R.I.T.S. stand for? To the members of our team, S.P.I.R.I.T.S. stands for integrity, trust, honesty, diligence, caring, and faith. This is what we want those who contact us seeking help with the paranormal to realize they can expect from us. This is what we hope our peers think of when they hear or see our teams' name. This is what is important to us. The reputation of our team that our name represents.

Many of the stories in this book are based on actual investigations of our *S.P.I.R.I.T.S. of New England* team, others are just complete fiction, but most include actual known haunted locations. Either way

I hope you enjoy them, and once you figure out which stories are which, be sure to check out our website at http://spiritsofnewengland.org to review the actual evidence from those stories that are based on our real investigations.

1
THE
FORGOTTEN
SOULS
OF
BAY PATH

Blessed are the poor in spirit: for theirs is the kingdom of heaven.
Matthew 5:3 – King James Version (KJV)

The S.P.I.R.I.T.S. of New England team had completed their investigation of the client's home in Springfield, Massachusetts two weeks earlier, and they were now nearly complete with review of the audio and video they had collected during the five-hour investigation, but after conducting numerous hours of research Jack found himself being lead in a direction he had not expected.

The client was a young man in his thirties, but he was very ill and the prognosis from his doctors was that it was terminal; this made it an urgent case for the team. The client had stated that he was seeing shadow figures in his home and that they were watching and following him even outside of the home. He had been touched, bruised, had objects move and heard scratching noises coming from the walls and ceilings of his bedroom. He heard both male and female voices talking and heard someone walking in the home when he knew he was alone. The team always took reports like this with some skepticism, but during this investigation just about every member of the team experienced what the client had stated was happening to him. Jack himself had witnessed a black shadow figure appear standing next to the couch he was sitting on right after feeling something grab and squeeze his leg. He had been conducting an EVP session in the basement apartment living room by himself while two of the other team members, Sharon and Sarah, were conducting an EVP session in the client's bedroom just down the hallway. Jack was asking who was trying to contact the client and demanded that they show themselves to him after he felt his leg being squeezed. He then heard an odd hissing noise that made him turn to his left and that's when he saw the figure standing next to the couch. It was so dark that it blocked out the picture that hung on the wall across from the couch. He tried to capture the figure on his IR camera but it did not show up on the IR, he could only see it with his own eyes, and then he watched it slowly fade away leaving behind only a cold spot that both he and Sarah were able to validate and follow around the room just moments after Jack saw the figure fade away. They also captured an EVP of a woman's voice saying "Didn't like me" just moments after the shadow figure had disappeared. The team also captured the sound of someone walking down the basement stairs, across the living room and down the hall towards the client's bedroom and also humming at the same time. This was also heard by Sarah and Sharon at the time it occurred, and it was so loud that they had called up to Jack at base camp to ask who had come down stairs. Jack informed them that no one had, and this was later confirmed by the DVR footage on the camera in the basement living room. No one had walked through at that time but the fact was that the footsteps and a woman humming were all captured on the audio of two different recorders setup in the living room and the client's bedroom. This was the first time the team had ever had so many experiences during one night's investigation and all of them validated the client's claims. They had even heard the scratching noises coming from the ceiling of the client's bedroom and tried to debunk it as some kind of animal but were not able to find anything to indicate an animal had gotten into the home.

One of the things that the client was adamant about to the team was the strange dreams he was having of people in dark cloaks and old style dress coming to visit him and just watching him. They would not talk to him, just watch him and stare at him. He was even beginning to see some of these people while he was awake, and it was scaring him as he did not understand what they wanted. The client stated that they would walk right through his walls but always from the same direction, from the east. In conducting his research Jack had found that there was an old pauper's cemetery not a quarter mile to the east from the client's home. The old cemetery was now named Bay Path and had been the official burial site for the old Springfield, MA Almshouse (Poor House) from 1873 – 1952 with over 1000 souls having been laid to rest there. They were all unmarked graves in that they were only provided with a number marker and even that was only in the later years of the cemetery, no grave stones with names were ever provided for the poor souls that were buried there. It was not until 1981 due to the tireless efforts of a concerned citizen and the Springfield Historical Society that the cemetery was finally cleaned up, fenced in, and a small monument head stone was placed in the cemetery to honor all of those buried there. Still, if there were restless souls from Bay Path visiting the client, then why? What was the connection between the client and these poor souls from the cemetery, if that was who was haunting him? Jack knew the team needed to find the connection if they were to help the client and he knew in his gut it meant making a trip to the old cemetery, and to gather more information from the client. Since time was urgent for this case, Jack decided to just take one other investigator with him to the cemetery as he would head out that same weekend. He contacted Sharon who agreed to go with him and let the rest of the team know what was going on.

It was late Sunday afternoon when Jack and Sharon arrived at Bay Path cemetery. They were shocked to see just how small it was considering that over one thousand people were buried there. It was not hard to imagine that over the seventy-nine years it was in use, and considering the lack of record keeping for it, that many grave plots had been used more than once, with bodies buried on top of bodies or even grave sites and their remains displaced or discarded to make room for a new occupant especially in the years between 1873 and the early 1900's. Even today the remains of the poor, destitute, and unwanted are not dealt with much better, for instance Jack found the current Massachusetts General Law in Part 1, Title XVI, Chapter 114, Section 43M on the Permanent Disposition of Dead Bodies or Remains, which states:

> "...Notwithstanding any general or special law to the contrary, a funeral establishment in possession of the cremated remains of a human body which is not claimed by a next-of-kin or duly authorized representative within 12 months after the date of cremation may have the remains interred or placed in a common grave, niche, or crypt in a cemetery, or scattered in an area of the cemetery designated for that purpose; provided, however, that if the deceased is a veteran of the United States Armed Forces the deceased shall be interred at a veterans' cemetery...."

After discovering this law and now staring woefully at the mass grave cemetery of Bay Path, Jack's only thought was that the States found a "cleaner" way to deal with the unwanted bodies of today's poor and destitute; burn them and scatter their ashes to the winds, stuff their ashes into a mass grave or some forgotten corner of a concrete crypt, nameless and again forgotten; just a nameless number input into a spreadsheet on some government computer, and most likely any name given to them would be Jane or John Doe as no one would bother to find out their real name anyway. Jack let out a deep sigh. Sharon came over to him after getting out of the truck.

"Jack, are you alright?"

Jack was leaning on the fence that enclosed the cemetery. He was starring off into the distance, but he did not need to look at Sharon to hear the genuine concern in her voice.

"Yeah. Yeah I'm fine. I was just thinking about all these poor souls that are buried here."

Sharon paused for a moment herself to reflect.

"Yeah, I just can't see how they could have buried over one thousand people in this small plot of land, how big do you think it is anyway?"

Jack sighed again.

"A bit over a quarter of an acre, not much more than that."

Sharon let out her own deep sigh.

"Jesus. How did they get all of those bodies in here?"

Jack turned and looked at her.

"It's basically a mass grave, bodies buried on top of bodies over the years."

Sharon winced at the thought, as that had not crossed her mind.

"God that's awful."

Jack could tell by her tone that Sharon was upset.

"Yeah it is."

Jack just looked at the ground and placed his right foot against the bottom of the chain link fence surrounding the cemetery.

"Well, let's see how to get into this place and try to figure out the connection to our client. Maybe there's something on the monument in there that will give us a clue. According to the cemetery's website the gate is supposed to be unlocked between 10 am and 6 pm every day, it's only going on 3 pm now but I see the gate is locked. I did try calling the grounds keeper before we got here but there was no answer. It looks like we may have to jump the fence."

Sharon was not keen on that idea, and neither was Jack, but they agreed there did not seem to be any other option. They checked around and found a low spot in the fence and climbed over. They walked to the flag pole at the north end where a patch of over grown thorn bushes also sat, they both assumed that somewhere in the tangle of the bushes was the small monument, they were right. There buried in the overgrowth of shrubs was a headstone. They could see there was some writing on it so Jack moved in and pushed away some of the overgrowth to reveal what was inscribed on the headstone.

BAY PATH
CEMETERY
1873-1954
BLESSED ARE THE POOR
IN SPIRIT FOR THEIRS IS
THE KINGDOM OF HEAVEN
MATH. 5:3
DEDICATED 1981
SPRINGFIELD
HISTORICAL SOCIETY

It was a nice gesture by the Springfield Historical Society, but it did not provide any answers or connection to the team's client, at least none that was obvious to Jack and Sharon. They both also doubted that it actually gave any peace to the souls that had been buried at Bay Path since there was actually no mention of them on the stone. Perhaps instead of mentioning the Historical Society they should have put on the stone "DEDICATED TO ALL THOSE BURIED HERE" or "IN LOVING MEMORY OF THOSE BURIED HERE", or anything that acknowledged all the nameless souls that lay in the cold earth beneath them. Jack was kneeling in front of the stone; he stood up and turned to Sharon.

"What do you think about conducting a short EVP session right here?"

Sharon did not hesitate in her response.

"That's a great idea! I have my recorder right here with me."

Jack smiled at her.

"So do I. Let's get started and see if we can't get some answers for our client."

They spent the next couple of hours asking questions near the head stone and in different parts of the small cemetery. Jack even asked some final questions on the outside of the fence before they got back in the truck and left. It was while asking a few questions and just talking to whatever spirits might be there that he thought he felt a presence near him and thought he felt someone touch him on his shoulder, this occurred when he asked if anyone there knew their client.

The next evening Jack and Sharon reviewed their audio. They captured only one EVP. It was caught on Jack's recorder just before they left the cemetery. It was one word in response to Jack's question of if anyone there knew their client. The word was "Kindred". Jack had remembered seeing the name on the map of the area when looking up the location of the cemetery. He pulled up the area again on Google maps and found what he was looking for. There on the map just south of Bay Path Cemetery was Kindred Hospital which is where their client had worked as a nurse, and also where he now went for his own medical treatments. This same location had also once been where the old Almshouse had stood, and by whom the old Potter's Field Cemetery, now called Bay Path Cemetery, was owned. This was the connection to their client, once a nurse who cared for the sick on the grounds where the Almshouse once stood. Somehow the spirits of that place had connected with him, perhaps they saw the client as someone who cared for people like themselves and now that he was facing his own mortality they were trying to connect with him, care for him in their own way, let him know that he is not alone and that death is not an end, it is a new beginning, and they will be there to help him pass into the next world when his time comes. His soul will not be one of the forgotten.

Bay Path is an actual cemetery located in Springfield, MA and the law quoted in this story is the actual law of the State of Massachusetts. The following photos are actual images of Bay Path Cemetery taken by the author.

Looking North: Bay Path Cemetery, Springfield, MA

Sign Installed by the State of Massachusetts in October 2000

The Actual Monument Dedicated by the Springfield Historical Society
in 1981

*"Yea, though I walk through the valley of the shadow of death,
I will fear no evil: for thou art with me..."*

Psalms 23:4 – King James Version (KJV)

2
GHOST SHIP

They that go down to the sea in ships and occupy their business in great waters: these men see the works of the Lord and his wonders in the deep. Psalm 107:23 – King James Version (KJV)

The ship sat docked in the Charlestown Navy Yard, it had been permanently stationed there since May of 1934. She was an old wooden Naval Frigate, built back in the late 1700's. She reached the pinnacle of her service during the War of 1812 where she defeated multiple enemy vessels, even when outnumbered. Many of her crew died on board, but not as much from combat as from disease, dysentery and drowning. It was these deaths that were the likely causes of the problems that affected the ships current crew, a crew of a new era, whose ships were now made of steel and filled with state of the art electronics and automated fire control systems. This new crew of the 21st century are not a superstitious lot, they do not believe in ghosts or demons, this new crew is a well-educated bunch of young people who were raised with the internet, cell phones and cable TV, but they also found it impossible to explain the things they were now experiencing on board their two-hundred-plus year old ship. A ship that is a throwback to a much simpler time, a ship without any fancy electronics except for the security system and a few lights which were installed in the 1970's. They had no explanation for their feelings of being watched on the ship at night while checking the bilge pump, or the disembodied footsteps on the ships wooden decks at night, or for the shadow figures they saw from time to time, or the voices they heard on the lower decks at night when they knew they were alone on the ship, or doors to the officers' quarters opening on their own. These were things that made them nervous, things they could not understand and the reason that their Commanding Officer agreed to his officers' request to contact a local paranormal team to come and investigate the ship for them to try and give them some answers.

The S.P.I.R.I.T.S. of New England team arrived at the Navy Yard just before dark, they were greeted by the ships Boatswain's Mate who helped them unload their gear and escorted them to the ship. The ship was intimidating in the dusk of night, with its black hull and white strip along the outer gun deck, and the dim lights from the inside gleaming through its cannon ports, the tall skeleton-like white masts reaching towards the quickly fading sky. They carried their gear up the wooden gangplank on the starboard side of the old ship. For as old as she was, the ship seemed eerily quiet, the wooden hull and deck under them did not seem to creak or groan at all like many old wooden ships do. The water in the bay was also dead calm, so there was not even the sound of any waves splashing against the ship's hull. The silence made Jack think of that line from the old western movies, just before the Indians attack, "It's quiet. Too quiet." Jack got a chill up his spine.

The setup took longer than they had hoped. The white painted walls of the inside decks played havoc with the IR cameras, causing terrible glare so it took some time to get the cameras adjusted properly. After about ninety minutes the team was finally ready to begin their investigation and the few lights on the ship were turned off. Except for the light on the Orlop deck where the bilge pump was located, as a crew member would need to check on it twice during the night. The other decks were dark in the blackness of the night, the only outside light was from the full moon that hovered in the star lit sky. Jack and Ellen were at base camp on the Orlop deck in the sail makers' room checking the final angles on the cameras. Jack grabbed his walkie and called the rest of the team members; Sharon, Sarah and Beck; who were on the gun deck and the berthing deck above them. Jack spoke quietly but with authority.

"Ladies, the cameras all look great so were ready to roll. Why don't you all head back here to base camp and we'll grab our gear, decide who's going where and get this investigation underway."

Sharon was the first to respond.

"Roger that. Beck and I are on our way."

"Sarah here. On my way as well."

Within a few moments everyone was back at base camp, Jack then turned to Ellen.

"Ok boss what's the plan?"

Ellen thought for a moment.

"Why don't Sharon and I head to the Surgeon's cockpit, where there are reports of hearing men talking, screams and moans. You and Beck head up to the Captain's quarters on the gun deck where there are reports of shadow figures and disembodied footsteps. Sarah can stay here and monitor the DVR system."

Jack nodded in agreement.

"That sounds good to me. What about you ladies?"

Jack turned and looked at the rest of the team. They all indicated their agreement with the plan. Sharon looked back at him and clapped her hands together.

"Ok, let's do it then!"

She was anxious to get started after the long setup, as was everyone else. It was now 10:30 pm. The fastest way to access the Surgeon's cockpit was to walk straight across the Orlop deck from base camp towards the stern of the ship. The cockpit was where terrible cramped and unsanitary conditions, along with poor lighting led to the loss of several crewmen whom died from complications during surgery after the battles were over. The room was small, only twelve-feet by nine-feet and about five-foot high from floor to ceiling. It was easier to sit down than try to crouch over in the room. The only other exit from the room was through the small stairway hatch that led up to the Midshipmen's Quarters on the Berthing deck. Like on all of the lower decks, if you needed to get out in a hurry, it just was not going to happen. Ellen and Sharon entered the small dark room, sat down in opposite corners and began their EVP session.

Jack and Beck had made their way back up through the main hatchways to the Gun deck and the Captain's Quarters/Map Room. There was a large table in the map room area and Jack setup their recorder on it. He also carried his hand held mini-dv with him and was recording all of their activities, even their journey back up through the ship. He was of the opinion that you just never know when paranormal activity might occur and you may capture something that you just did not notice at the time. On the way up he and Beck decided to just try and speak to any spirits that might be on the ship, but they would use the language and terms from the old sailing ship days of the 1800's to try and communicate. The room was dark except for some residual light coming through the gun ports. Jack yelled out into the darkness of the Gun deck.

"All crewmembers report to the Map room, on the double!"

There was silence for several minutes neither investigator moved or spoke. Then Jack noticed that Beck was staring at the starboard door entrance to the Map room. She seemed bewildered, confused. He spoke quietly to her.

"What's wrong Beck?"

Beck stammered.

"I...I thought I saw a face in the door. It was the face of a boy."

Jack had been facing the other direction filming into the Captain's room. He questioned her further.

"Where did you see it?"

Beck pointed at the door.

"In that doorway over to our right."

The door was not closed completely; it was open about 4 inches.

"It looked like a young boy, his face peeking through the door."

Beck was more firm now with what she had seen. Jack walked over to the door and opened it further, stepping out onto the Gun deck.

"Hello! Who's out here?"

He spoke firmly and with authority. Then he saw movement. A dark shadow figure darted across the Gun deck in front of him moving left to right. It startled him and he pulled back although he kept the mini-dv up and filming and pointed it to where the figure had moved. There was nothing in the camera's viewfinder but one of the cannons. Jack moved towards it, Beck followed him.

"Jack, did you just see that?"

Beck's voice was shaking.

"Yeah I saw it. It was a shadow figure. It went to the cannon."

Jack looked to the cannon where they saw the shadow move to.

"Beck there's nothing there. There's no place for anyone to hide there."

Beck stayed close to Jack, then without warning, the starboard door they had just come through slammed with a bang behind them, followed by the eerie laugh of a young boy. They both jump at the slam of the door and a terrible cold chill ran through them as the disembodied laugh echoed through the Gun deck.

Ellen and Sharon had only just begun their EVP session when they heard the sounds of someone walking on the deck above them and the sounds of furniture moving. Ellen turned to Sharon.

"Isn't that the Berthing deck above us?"

Sharon responded.

"No, that's the Midshipmen's Quarters to be exact. But there shouldn't be anyone up there. Unless we're hearing Jack and Beck, but they should be another deck up. Those sounds are right over our heads!"

Sharon slowly stood up and moved towards the ladder hatchway leading up to the Midshipmen's Quarters. She slowly and quietly moved her way up the ladder, just enough to poke her head onto the next deck and look around. Ellen stood up and moved quietly towards Sharon.

"Sharon do you see anything?"

They could still hear the footsteps, but it was almost pitch black on the next deck and Sharon could not see anything although she could hear someone walking around, then the sound of wood on wood, like a chair being dragged across the deck. Sharon pulled out her mini-flashlight, clicked it on and pointed it in the direction the sounds were coming from. There in her light was a black human shaped figure standing by a small round table with several chairs around it. The figure suddenly darted back from the light and a chair went flying at Sharon's head! She immediately ducked out of instinct, but lost her footing and tumbled down the ladder and into Ellen. The two women recovered themselves quickly and Sharon shined her light up into the hatchway. There at the top of the hatchway; seeming to be glaring down at them; was the black shadow figure.

Sarah jumped from her seat at the monitor when she heard the scream, it was followed by loud banging and crashing and then the heavy footfalls of someone running across one of the decks. Sarah stepped out from the small room and onto the Orlop deck, she could see Ellen moving quickly towards her. Sarah yelled to her.

"What's going on!? Is everyone ok!?"

Ellen yelled back to her. Sarah could see her mother was worried and a bit frantic.

"Sarah! Check the monitor quick! Do you see Sharon on any of the cameras!?"

Sarah stepped back into the small room and began scanning the four camera views.

"Yes! I see her on camera 4 on the berthing deck! She…She's just standing there, staring… I don't…"

Then Sarah spotted what Sharon was staring at. It was just off to the left side of the camera view, a tall dark shadow figure, just standing there, seeming to stare back at Sharon. The scene sent chills up Sarah's spine. It was like watching some kind of paranormal Mexican standoff.

"Sarah!"

Ellen's voice snapped at her.

"Get Jack on the radio and tell him to make his way down to Sharon. Tell him to do it quickly but quietly. I'm hoping we can corner this thing."

Sarah jumped at her mother's tone.

"Ok, but who screamed? I heard someone scream!"

Ellen could see that Sarah was a bit shaken, and she was concerned that what she was about to tell her would freak her out even more.

"That scream you heard came from that shadow figure when Sharon shined her UV light on it."

Sarah's face turned ashen but she kept to the plan and called Jack on the walkie. Jack and Beck were still on the main gun deck trying to get whatever had just interacted with them to do it again. The odd disembodied laugh had sent chills through them both but they were more excited about it than frightened by it. The sudden sound of Sarah's voice through the walkie startled them both. Jack unclipped it from his belt.

"Sarah this is Jack what's up?"

Sarah depressed the button on her walkie, leaning close into it she spoke softly and as calmly as she could muster.

"Ellen needs you to make your way down to the berthing deck as quick as you can, but you need to be as quiet as possible."

Neither Jack nor Beck had heard the scream and had no idea what had just taken place on the lower deck. They immediately got the hint from Sarah's tone that something serious was taking place. Jack kept his own voice low in response.

"Why what's going on?"

"Ellen and Sharon had an encounter with a shadow person. Sharon is still with it right now on the berthing deck. I can see them on the camera. Jack this thing screamed when Sharon shined her UV light on it. I remember what you told me about negative entities not liking UV light…"

Jack cut her off.

"Ok Sarah, I'm heading down there now, but where exactly are Sharon and this figure on that deck?"

Sarah looked back at the monitor to try and give Jack her best assessment of exactly where Sharon and the figure were.

"They're about in the middle of the deck. I can see a stairway just behind the dark figure. It's the stairway closer to the bow of the ship."

Jack thought for a moment, running the layout of the ship through his head based on where he currently was standing.

"Ok, I got it. The berthing deck is just below us here so I'll make my way towards that stairway and come down behind it. I'm on my way."

He then realized that Sharon also had a walkie on her and could probably hear their conversation.

"Sharon if you heard us just nod and Sarah will let me know."

Sarah was still watching the monitor while listening to Jack.

"Jack, Sharon is nodding. She heard you."

"Excellent. Sharon, I'm on my way."

Jack then turned to Beck. He could see she was nervous and a bit confused. He clipped his walkie back onto his belt, then reached into his coat pocket and pulled out a flashlight. He grabbed Beck's hand and slapped the flashlight into it.

"Beck stay here, take my UV light, if that shadow figures comes up here just shine this light on it, it will chase it away. For whatever reason negative entities hate UV light, it seems to hurt them. Just stay in the Map Room, you'll be fine."

Beck did not like the idea of being left alone, but she was also thankful that this time Jack had not asked her to go with him. It was not because she was afraid to go, she would not hesitate if she asked him to, she just still was not sure what exactly was happening, she had not had time to absorb it all, so she was not sure what help she would be.

"Ok, you got it, but if you need me just yell."

Jack nodded, then turned and headed quietly down the gun deck to the berthing deck hatchway. He stopped at the opening. He pulled a second flashlight from his coat pocket, but this was just a normal white light, not a UV light. If it really was a negative entity this was not going to protect him, he knew that, but he could still use it before he stepped down to signal Sharon he was coming. He clicked it on and off once and then started down the stairway as quietly as possible. He was halfway down when he heard Sharon whisper to him.

"Jack, don't move. Can you see it? I think it heard you. It's right at the bottom of the stairs in front of you."

Jack peered down into the darkness. It took his eyes a moment to adjust and then he saw it. It was darker than the dark. It seemed to be trying to intimidate him, to scare him away, but Jack was not leaving and neither was Sharon. Jack sat down on the steps. The shadow figure moved closer to the stairs. Jack just sat there, motionless, watching to see what it might do next. It just stood there at the base of the stairs. Jack finally spoke.

"Who are you?"

Jack had his Real-Time EVP recorder and his earbuds with him, and had been using them the whole investigation. He had the recorder set for a ten-second delay and listened intently for any reply. Nothing.

"Why are you here?"

This time he heard a rough whispery voice say "Watch". Jack thought for a moment before responding.

"Do you mean you watch over the ship?"

No reply. He asked the same question again.

"Do you watch the ship?"

Another whispery reply.

"Yes."

Jack let out a sign. He needed to collect his thoughts before asking his next question. Depending on the reply, if any, he needed to know what he would say next.

"Do you want us to leave?"

He got the reply he expected.

"Yes."

Jack responded without hesitation, but he spoke slowly and deliberately.

"We can't leave. We have orders from the Captain to be here, to find out who is on this ship. We can't leave until we complete our mission. Do you understand?"

This time there was no reply. The figure just stood there, staring back at Jack. Then Sharon piped in. Although she had not heard the replies Jack had gotten, she was able to infer from his questions and responses what was going on.

"You have to tell us who you are or we can't leave."

Jack listened intently, but there was nothing and he shook his head so Sharon would know. Sharon asked another question.

"If you're here to guard this ship, why did this light hurt you?"

Sharon held out the UV light she had in her hand, as if to show it to the apparition. Jack heard a clear response this time, it was a male voice.

"No."

Jack followed quickly with another question.

"No? Do you mean the light did not hurt you?"

The same male voice responded again.

"No."

Jack followed up quickly.

"Then why did you scream?"

Jack had been staring at the shadow figure when he noticed Sharon standing with her hands on her hips, looking a bit frustrated. He understood her frustration and was about to clue her in on what was being said when a reply to his last question came through. It was a completely unexpected response, and it caught him off guard.

"Scare."

His reaction to the entities answer was just a reflex, as well as induced from all of the built up anxiety, stress, and the late hour after a long setup for the investigation. Jack, began to laugh. Not just a simple "ha-ha" funny kind of laugh, but a deep, breath taking, make you cry kind of laugh. Sharon looked at him confused and more than a little aggravated.

"What the hell is so funny!?"

Jack was still laughing. He could not help himself. He could see Sharon was getting angry. He let out a deep sigh and then took a deep breath to compose himself, as he did the figure began to fade away before their eyes. Sharon noticed it first.

"Jack look! It's fading away!"

Jack took another deep breath and let it out.

"Ahhh...yeah...well I'm not surprised. I'm sure I just either embarrassed it or upset it."

Sharon looked puzzled, and still annoyed.

"What do you mean?"

Jack was finally able to compose himself and began to explain.

"Well based on the replies I got, it's here to keep watch over the ship. It thought we didn't belong here and it screamed at you to try and scare you away, not because of the UV light."

Sharon began laughing having been let in on the joke so to speak.

"Hahahahahaha! That ghost knows better now than to try and scare us off! Hell that's what we're here for! To make contact, to talk to it!"

Jack gave a big smile.

"Yeah, well I think you may have frightened it a bit when you chased after it rather than running away from it!"

The two investigators could not stop laughing. Beck, Ellen and Sarah heard them and came to see what the hell was going on. Jack and Sharon explained what had happened and they all listened back to the audio with the EVP responses. It was like nothing they had ever experienced before, but it was comical as well. A spirit had tried to scare them off and in the process they collected some of the best evidence they ever had, and ended up chasing off the spirit.

Before the night was out though, they apologized as a group to the spirit for what had happened, and informed any spirits on board that they would be back for a second night's investigation by request of the current Captain. The second night was even more eventful than the first with much more activity and EVPs being captured. They never did get a name of who was on board, but they did get an EVP telling them "Your welcome back".

Several weeks later all of the evidence was presented to the Captain and the ships officers which, for them at least, validated their experiences and put them all a little more at ease that the spirits are there to keep a watchful eye over the ship and the crew. The U.S.S. Constitution was and is their home and they are there to protect it.

The U.S.S. Constitution (Old Iron Sides) is the oldest commissioned active naval ship in the world. She was named by President George Washington after the Constitution of The United States, and was authorized for construction along with five other war frigates under the Naval Act of 1794. She was the third of the six built and was launched in 1797. She was built in the Charlestown Navy Yard in Charlestown, MA and is still berthed there today. The Constitution is best remembered for her actions during the War of 1812 and her successful battles against five British Warships the HMS Guerriere, Java, Pictou, Cyane, and Levant. In 2010 she was declared Ship of State by act of Congress, and in 2015 she began undergoing major restoration in dry dock. In July 2017 all restoration was completed after 26 months in dry dock. A little after 11:00 pm on 23 July 2017 The U.S.S. Constitution quietly re-entered the waters of Boston Harbor and returned to her permanent home berth adjacent to Dry Dock 1 in the Charlestown Navy Yard.

In July of 2010 *S.P.I.R.I.T.S. of New England* was requested by the Commander of the U.S.S. Constitution to conduct a paranormal investigation of the ship due to numerous reports of paranormal activity by the ships' crew. S.P.I.R.I.T.S. was allowed two full nights to investigate the ship and was given full access to the entire ship. From July of 2010 until 2016, *S.P.I.R.I.T.S. of New England* was the first and only paranormal team in the world to investigate the U.S.S. Constitution. In 2016 it was re-investigated by Mr. Jason Hawes and his team for the television show Ghost Hunters, the episode aired 11 November 2016. The following are just of few of the photos that were taken by the author Jack Kenna, during S.P.I.R.I.T.S. investigation of the ship in 2010.

To learn more about the U.S.S. Constitution; "Old Ironsides"; or to plan a visit go to https://ussconstitutionmuseum.org .

The U.S.S. Constitution – 2:00 AM 26 July 2010

Main Gun Deck of the U.S.S. Constitution

The Tiller Room

S.P.I.R.I.T.S. team member Sarah Campbell conducting an EVP session in the belly of the ship, the original gun powder room.

The Officers' Quarters on the Birthing Deck where dis-embodied footsteps were heard, shadow figures seen, EVPs were captured, and a truly paranormal anomaly was captured on video by the S.P.I.R.I.T.S. team.

With deepest thanks to the U.S. Navy and the 2010 Commander and Crew of the U.S.S. Constitution and to all those who serve our great nation at sea.

THE ORIGINAL 1861 NAVY HYMM

COMPOSED BY REV. JOHN BACCHUS DYKES
AN ENGLISH EPISCOPALIAN CLERGYMAN

Eternal Father, strong to save,
Whose arm hath bound the restless wave,
Who bidd'st the mighty ocean deep
Its own appointed limits keep;
Oh, hear us when we cry to Thee,
For those in peril on the sea!

O Christ! Whose voice the waters heard
And hushed their raging at Thy word,
Who walked'st on the foaming deep,
And calm amidst its rage didst sleep;
Oh, hear us when we cry to Thee,
For those in peril on the sea!

Most Holy Spirit! Who didst brood
Upon the chaos dark and rude,
And bid its angry tumult cease,
And give, for wild confusion, peace;
Oh, hear us when we cry to Thee,
For those in peril on the sea!

O Trinity of love and power!
Our brethren shield in danger's hour;
From rock and tempest, fire and foe,
Protect them wheresoe'er they go;
Thus evermore shall rise to Thee
Glad hymns of praise from land and sea!

3

FROGS IN THE CLOSET

And if thou refuse to let them go, behold, I will smite all thy borders with frogs... Exodus 8:2 – King James Version (KJV)

The house sat high on the hill along with many others above the Merrimack River. The homes on the hill were old, many built in the early to late 1800's, some were even older their architecture attesting to their age. Most homes had been built upon the hills in the area due to the firm foundation of granite under the soil, as compared to the muddy clay of the valley lands below. In the old days the river often flooded as well which brought the problems of not only loosing once home, but possibly one's life. This was now the 21st century and those problems had long since been engineered away and the river was much better controlled. The houses on the hill now were more sought after for their views of the river than protection from it. For Maria Rodriguez and her family though, the view from their home on the hill provided no comfort just as living on it provided no protection from thing that plagued them.

It was either very late or very early Maria was thinking as she laid wide awake in bed. Her clock showed 3:00 am. The storm outside was still raging. Lightening flashed, thunder roared, and the winds not only howled but shook the house as they gusted down through the river valley and over the top of the hill. The storm was not what kept her awake though. For several weeks since they had first moved in, her youngest daughter Lacey was being terrified by something she said was hiding in her closet. It would talk to her at night from inside the closet. Both Maria and her son each saw her sitting on the floor in front of her closet nodding her head, and seeming to be having a conversation with someone. Later Maria asked her who she was talking to in her room and Lacey told her it was the ugly green boy who lives in her closest. It all seemed innocent enough in the beginning, but over the last couple of weeks things took a dark turn and Lacey was now afraid to stay in her own room. The rest of the family were also experiencing things they could not explain. Maria, her eighteen-year-old son David, and her two teenage daughters Renata, sixteen and Mia, fourteen; all had seen a tall dark shadow figure in Mia's bedroom and the upstairs hallway. They all were woken at night by their beds shaking, and they all saw bright flashes of white light in almost every room in the house that they could not find an explanation for. The light always seemed to emanate from inside the house, and seemed like a flash of lightening, but there was no storm.

There was a large bright flash of light, followed by a low rumbling that grew into a loud crash, the storm startled Maria from her thoughts, but the high pitched screamed that followed sent chills through her and created a feeling of panic and dread. She threw off her covers, sprang from her bed, and ran from her room towards the stairs to the second floor.

"Lacey! Baby I'm coming!"

Lights in each upstairs bedroom of the house came on as Laceys' brother and sisters all woke up to come to her aid as her screams continued. Her fourteen-year-old sister Mia was first to reach her. She stopped dead in the doorway to Laceys' room, her mind unable to totally comprehend the small black figure with the glowing yellow eyes crouching by the closet door. Lacey was in a fetal position on the floor, her eyes shut tight, her mouth wide open as she screamed at the top of her lungs, her blankets half wrapped around her as if she had been yanked out of her bed. Mia was terrified, she knew she was screaming, but there was nothing coming out, she took deep breath and tried again....

"MOM!!!!!!!!!"

Even the loud clap of thunder that accompanied Mia's scream could not drown it out, as the rage of the storm seemed to mimic the insane nature of what was happening inside the home.

Ellen and Sharon had worked at Brigham & Women's Hospital in Boston together for many years. It is where they first met long before they had ever founded their paranormal team S.P.I.R.I.T.S. of New England. As usual they were having lunch together, but of late their discussions were more about their paranormal cases than anything work related. Today was no different, but today what Ellen need to discuss with Sharon was extremely urgent.

"Sharon, Jack called me this morning with a new case. A family up in Haverhill is claiming to be experiencing some pretty intense activity that is affecting the whole family, but it seems to be focused mostly on the woman's four-year-old daughter."

Sharon could tell by the look in Ellen's face and the tone in her voice it was a case they were going to need to move on right away.

"So what's happening?"

For the next ten minutes Ellen went on to explain what the family had been experiencing, and the final straw during last night's storm that had driven the family to seek out a paranormal team to help them. Ellen took out a copy of their client information form that Maria Rodriguez had filled out on the teams' website and emailed to them. They went over all of the reported activity of the family's beds shaking, the strange flashes of bright white light in the upstairs bedrooms, the ugly little green boy in Laceys' closet, and also the supposed negative history of the house having once been owned by a woman practicing black witchcraft and the witch's husband committing suicide by hanging himself in one of the closets of the upstairs bedrooms, the room that now belonged to Mia. The witch supposedly went mad after that and shot herself in the home. Sharon paused for a moment to take it all in.

"Wholly crap Ellen! That sounds like it could be demonic!"
Ellen nodded in agreement.

"I know. I said that to Jack as well. I told him I wasn't sure we should take this case."
Sharon now had on her poker face.

"Well, what does Jack think? How did he respond to you thinking we should pass on it?"
Sharon was already pretty sure she knew basically what Jack would have said, but she wanted to hear it from Ellen.

"You know Jack, what do you think he said? He told me not to jump to conclusions about it being demonic, but he understands my concerns and we will of course take precautions. If anything doesn't seem right, we can always call our demonologist friend's Katie and Beckah for help."
Sharon smiled.

"Yep, that sounds like our Jack! So when do we go?"
Ellen knew Sharon would be happy hearing that. Sharon and Jack were somewhat alike, in that they loved to dive into cases head first. They loved the challenge, the adventure, and wanted with all their hearts to help people. She on the other hand was the teams' protector, the worrying mother, always trying to watch out for everyone, and yes, especially her own daughter Sarah who was on the team. She wanted to help these people, help them figure out what was going on, but not if it meant putting her extended family in harm's way of a true demonic spirit. She would prefer they turn

something like that over to someone who was a demonologist.

"Jack wants to go this coming Saturday. He already set it up with the family given the urgency of the case. So we have five days to prepare at least. Are you good with this Saturday Sharon?"

Sharon gave a big smile.

"Yep! I'm good to go, so let Jack know."

Ellen sat back in her chair.

"Okay, but for now we better finish up lunch and get back to work. I'll send out the email confirming Saturday's investigation latter."

That Saturday the team arrived at the family's home. While Sharon and Sarah began to setup some of the teams' equipment; Ellen, Jack and Beck sat down in the living room with the family to discuss what they were experiencing, and where most of the activity was taking place. Ellen sat next to Maria on the couch. Lacey was in Maria's lap, her son sat next to her, and the teenage girls sat on the floor by the coffee table to the right of their mother. Jack sat in an old recliner chair in one corner of the room near a front window of the house, he had placed an audio recorder on the coffee table to capture the conversation for reference later. Beck sat in another at the opposite end of the living from Jack. Ellen spoke first.

"So tell us about your most recent experiences in the house. Have you had any others since the night of the storm?"

Maria was visibly nervous; she did not really want to talk about these experiences. She had grown up in a strict catholic family, and they did not believe in such things as ghosts. People who did were just crazy and to be ignored or shunned. Not until these things began happening to her and her family did she believe they could be real, but still to talk about them and yet again now believe in them, it went against everything she had been taught and believed. Jack could see the distress on her face.

"Maria."

Jack spoke reassuringly.

"You're catholic correct? That's what you filled out on your form."

She smiled and looked up at him.

"Yes."

Jack leaned forward with his elbows on his knees, his forearms extended out and his hands open. This was to indicate to Maria that it was okay to talk to them in person about what was going on, that they will listen to her and were not there to judge her. He smiled back at her.

"I'm also catholic. Believe me I know our faith's beliefs; I know some of the stigma associated with it regarding ghosts or spirits. Since I was a kid I have seen and experienced things that I can't explain. We have helped many people of many different faiths experiencing things like this. We are the ones you can talk to about it and we don't judge you or think you're crazy. You can talk with us. We are here to help."

Maria smiled again and gave Lacey a hug and a kiss on her forehead. The little girl squirmed for a moment, then hugged her mother back.

"Thank you Jack. Thank all of you for coming here to help us. It is difficult for me to talk about, but we're so glad you're all here. Well, two nights ago we were all sitting at the kitchen table playing cards when we suddenly heard what sounded like a child running around upstairs in the bedrooms."

Ellen knew it was unlikely a four-year-old would be sitting with them at night playing cards.

"Where was Lacey at the time?"

Maria was a bit annoyed by the question. Did not Ellen think she would know if it was her own daughter running around upstairs? She kept her composure and answered Ellen's question.

"She was sleeping in my bedroom down here off the kitchen. She will no longer sleep in her own room after this last incident during the storm."

Jack noticed the look on Maria's face as she answered. She did not seem happy with the question.

"Maria, I know some of our questions may seem a bit ridiculous at times, but as an investigation team we have to ask them in order to gather all the facts to help you and your family. We wouldn't be doing our job right if we didn't ask the questions, but if we do ask something you feel is over the top or you just don't want to answer it that's okay just tell us you don't want to answer it."

Beck chimed in as well with her unmistakable southern accent.

"That's right, if Jack or any of us step over the line you just smack him. Jack that is, not the rest of us, but you have our permission to smack him."

As usual Beck knew exactly when and how to break the tension in the room and calm people's nerves. Everyone began to laugh. After a moment, Ellen asked if there was anything else she wanted to tell them before the investigation began. Maria thought for a moment.

"Well you know that Lacey sees this ugly little green boy in her closet. He talks to her. Me and my son have seen her talking to the closet, but I we had never seen anyone there. At least not until the night of the storm when my daughter Mia saw it."

Maria pointed to her fourteen-year-old sitting on the floor to her right. Mia went on to explain to the team what she had seen that night, and how it seemed to change from a solid dark figure into a black misty kind of thing that just vanished into the shadows of the closet. She was visibly shaking while describing it, and her voice choked up at times while she tried to speed-talk her way through the event just to get it out of the way and out of her mind. She did not like talking about it, it still terrified her, and that was painfully obvious to everyone in the room.

"Wow, I can only imagine how horrifying that must have been for you."

Sharon's voice startled everyone in the room. They were all listening so intently to Mia, they had not seen or heard her come in and stand in the doorway to the living room. Ellen was the first to react.

"Jesus Sharon! Make some noise next time will ya!"

Sharon laughed and smiled, as did everyone else, including Ellen.

"Sorry everyone. I had just come down to let you know Sarah and I have pretty much finished setting up all the equipment. Jack do you want to come into the kitchen and check out the angels on the DVR cameras?"

Although Sharon was the teams' equipment manager, Jack was the teams' technical expert, he also typically lead each investigation for the team as his personal skills were very strong in both of those areas. In his day job he was a Senior Engineering Technician for the Department of Defense. He had been responsible for running projects and managing teams most of his career, and just happened to have a knack for it.

"Yep, okay let's go check it out. The rest of you can stay here and chat for now, this won't take long."

Jack had Sarah made a couple minor adjustments to two of the four infrared night vision cameras, but for the most part they were good to go. They had one camera at the top of the landing to the second floor bedrooms looking down the hallway so you could see each bedroom door, and the bathroom door at the end of the hall. Then there was one in Renata's room setup in the front left corner of the room so you could see her door, bed, closet, and window. In Mia's room it was setup looking toward the door to her room so you could see her closet door, bed and most of the bedroom. The last camera was setup in Laceys' room in the front right corner of the room looking towards the closet where the ugly little green boy came from, and where Mia had seen the shadow figure with the yellow glowing eyes.

Jack leaned back from the chair in front of the monitor that was hooked into the DVR cameras. All four cameras were up and running and recording.

"Looks good to me Sharon. What do you think?"

Sharon knew it was really just a rhetorical question. Sometimes she thought that Jack just liked to hear himself talk. She smiled.

"Enough of the BS, let's get this party started!"

Jack smiled back, sat back up in the chair, stood up and stretched.

"You're the boss."

They turned and went back into the living room to let everyone know they were ready to get started with the investigation. Ellen was answering a question for the family when Jack and Sharon walked in, followed by Sarah.

"To answer your questions about spirits, yes if they have enough energy they can move things, make noises, and even show themselves to you, but until we complete our investigation I don't want to say that it's a spirit that's shaking your beds, it could be something non-paranormal that's causing that. I do find the lights to be odd though. We will do our best to figure those out for you. It could be car headlights reflecting into the windows, or street lights, or something else."

Beck had been watching Ellen as she spoke, listening. When Ellen was done she turned her attention to the family.

"I agree with Ellen. We just don't know for sure yet what's really happening here but, hopefully, we will have some answers for you very soon."

Maria smiled back at both them, she was still holding Lacey on her lap.

"Thank you Ellen and Beck. Thank all of you for doing this for us. We are at our wits end."

Jack spoke up from the doorway.

"No worries Maria, that's what we're here for. To help."

Jack clapped his hands together to make sure he had everyone's attention.

"Okay, so all of the cameras and recorders are setup and ready to go. We are ready to get started and see what we can find out for you. The only thing left to do is for us to throw you out of your own home for the rest of the night."

He smiled. Maria smiled back. Beck looked up at him from her chair shaking her head, and musing to herself.

"You're such a Jerk."

Jack's smile got bigger, Sharon, Sarah and Ellen all laughed. Maria and her family did not understand it, but Jack did. He knew that "Jerk" was just a term of endearment that his team mates used for him, even when he sometimes was being one. It was a name that a famous investigator friend of theirs had somewhat inadvertently baptized him with in front of his team at a paranormal event on the ship the USS Salem. He knew he would never live it down so he decided to own the term, and occasionally try to live up to it for them.

The family had made arrangements to stay with some friends for the night while the S.P.I.R.I.T.S. team investigated their home. The team would be there until the early hours of the morning as was typical for any investigation they did. This would give them enough time to try and experience the family's claims and/or to find more natural causes for them, or so call "debunk" their experiences. Ellen and Sharon spent some time conducting a baseline Electromagnetic Field (EMF) sweep of the home and found unusually high EMF readings in the vertical direction of the home, the average being 2.5 milligauss. The odd thing about these readings was that they consistently occurred on every level of the home but no exact source or sources could be identified for these readings.

Jack, Sarah and Beck spent the time preparing the hand-held IR cameras and digital recorders they would carry with them during the investigation. All of the equipment was outfitted with new batteries, and each had plenty of hours of recording time. It was time to break up into teams and leave someone at the monitor to keep an eye on what was happening on the DVR cameras. Each team and the person at the monitor would be equipped with a walkie-talkie to stay in communication with each other. Ellen look around at her team.

"Okay is everyone ready to get started? Its 9:20 pm, the family has left for the night so we should get our investigation underway. Where does everyone want to start?"

All heads turned to Jack. It used to bother him a bit, everyone looking to him for the game plan. It bothered him originally because it was not his team, he was the late comer to the group, not a founding member. He felt like he was stepping on peoples' toes, but over the years he had gotten used to it. It had just become a natural way the team functioned, and it worked very well. Everyone on the team had their own skills they brought to the table, organizing and knowing the tech stuff were Jack's.

"I'll be the first to stay here at basecamp and monitor the DVR cameras. Ellen you and Sharon take Laceys' room, Beck you and Sarah…."

Sarah interrupted. She had something on her mind that she wanted to try herself.

"If it's okay, I would like to investigate Mia's room on my own for the first hour. I'll keep a walkie with me and you can keep an eye on me on the DVR system. I want to try and make contact with the man who killed himself in that room."

Jack was a bit surprised by Sarah's request. It was a breach of protocol. No one was to investigate alone, and for many obvious reasons; injury, validation of an experience or event, fear reduction, etc. Jack looked to Ellen.

"Well, it's not typical protocol, but the location is pretty condensed, we have a DVR camera in that room, she will have a walkie on her, and you ladies will be in the room right across the hall, so what do you think?"

Sarah could see her mother was not happy with the idea. Even though Sarah was twenty-three, she knew she was still her mother's little girl, but she also knew her mother trusted her, she was just very protective of her. That was when Beck spoke up.

"Let her do it Ellen. The girl is twenty-three years old, and besides she'll be right across the hall from us."

Ellen glared at Beck and then at Sarah.

"Okay. Fine. But I don't really like it, and you are to leave the door to that room open! Understand?"

Sarah gave her typical I got my way smile.

"Yes ma'am. Not a problem."

Jack looked at Sharon, he now had a small dilemma. What to do with the Sharon. Beck spoke up again and solved Jack's problem for him.

"I'll stay here with Jack for now and maybe investigate Maria's bedroom or the living room on this floor."

Jack looked up at Beck and smiled, then he turned to the rest of the team.

"Okay then. So Sarah you're in Mia's room, and Ellen and Sharon you're in Laceys' room. Do what you can to make contact with that ugly little green boy. Sarah, be careful and just keep that walkie handy. Now go get started!"

He waved his right hand at them as if shooing away flies. The three headed upstairs and Beck headed into Maria's bedroom off from the kitchen.

Sarah entered Mia's room and found herself a spot on the floor next to the bed, facing the closet door and where she could also see the door to the hallway. She sat with her back resting against the bed and her legs crossed. She had placed a KII meter on the floor about three feet in front of her, so it was between her and the closet door. She was holding a digital recorder to try and capture any EVP's as she attempted to communicate with the spirit of the man who had hung himself. She did a radio check with Jack to make sure her walkie was working properly and to follow up with staying in communication as she had promised. She also had to admit to herself that she was a bit nervous being in the room by herself given the reported activity and not knowing what to expect, but this is something she wanted to try and was determined to do it. Sarah was sensitive to energies, including spirit energies, but for the moment the room did not seem to reveal anything to her. It just felt like any other room. She began her EVP session. She spoke softly.

"I'm looking to speak with the man who died here. I have a device on the floor in front of me, if you touch it or use your energy you can make it light up to talk with me."

The KII is a type of EMF meter that has five lights at the top of it. Each light represents a range level of EMF, and the higher the EMF the more lights that will light up. Paranormal investigators use this device as a means to potentially allow spirits to communicate with them by making the lights on the device flash for yes or no. In this instance the KII Sarah was using did nothing in response to her statement, but then again it was a statement and not a question.

"I want to ask you some questions if that's okay. We want to understand who you are and help you if you need it."

Again, nothing on the KII. This did not necessarily mean that she was not getting any interaction. She did have the audio recorder, so it was possible she was maybe getting an EVP or two, so she was careful to leave about ten seconds between her questions for any potential reply from a spirit to be recorded.

"Are you the man who hung himself in this room?"

"Was the woman you lived with a witch?"

"Did she drive you to kill yourself?"

"Do you need help?"

The KII meter remained silent. Sarah stopped the audio recorder and held it to her ear as she played it back listening for any possible answers to her questions, she received two! This is what Sarah heard.
(Sarah's second question)
"...Was the woman who lived with you a witch?"
(Male voice response)
"Yesss."
(Sarah's last question)
"...Do you need help?"
(Male voice response)
"Yesss."
Just then Sarah's attention was captured by a quick flash of the lights on the KII meter. Her head snapped up to look at it.

"That's right, use the KII meter to communicate with me."
The KII flashed again, and it was at that moment Sarah heard the latch on the closet door click. She looked up from the KII and saw the closet door begin to slowly open, and a dark mass seemed to begin to creep out from inside the darkness of the closet. Sarah froze in place, but she did not panic. She hoped Jack was watching her on the monitor, and she kept her left hand firmly on the walkie just in

case. She took a deep breath and let it out slowly to calm herself. She stayed still and spoke gently to the dark figure emerging from the closet.

"I can see you. It's okay, we are here to help you if you need it, but you need to keep communicating with me."

The KII flashed twice this time.

"That's right, use the KII meter."

Ellen and Sharon had settled into Laceys' which was just on the opposite side of the hallway from Mia's room. Ellen was sitting on the bed near the entrance door to the room, while Sharon sat on the floor at the foot of the bed directly across from the closet on the opposite side of the room. Sharon had placed a KII meter just in front of the closet whose door was about a third of the way open. They had begun their EVP session just about the same time Sarah began hers.

"Hello, my name is Ellen and this is Sharon. We are here to talk with you tonight. Lacey and her family asked us to come here and talk with you. There is a little gray box on the floor in front of you. You can touch it and make it light up to talk with us. It won't harm you. Make it light up once for yes, and don't do anything for no. Do you understand?"

The KII flashed once. Ellen leaned forward, it always intrigued her to see potential interaction on the KII. Sharon was more skeptical and reserved her reaction until she received more than one response. Sharon asked the next question.

"So there is someone else here in the room with us?

The KII immediately flashed again. Ellen followed up.

"Are you a child?"

Again, it flashed just once for "yes".

"Are you a little girl?"

This time the meter remained silent. Sharon asked the next one.

"Are you a little boy?"

Immediately the KII light up all six lights and held there for just a moment.

"Well I would say that was a definite YES."

Both Ellen and Sharon were excited at this point. This seemed to be real direct communication with a spirit in the house. Ellen's mind was humming now, she wanted answers for the family.

"Are you the little boy that talks to Lacey?"
The KII flashed again. Both Ellen and Sharon were a bit dumbfounded now, this was not just coincidence or some type of man-made interference, this was direct communication. Sharon decided to change tactics a bit and see if she could illicit a bit stronger, or at least different, response from whomever they were communicating with.

"Lacey says you're an ugly little green boy. Why are you green? Are you a frog?"
Her idea had been to just try a mild form of antagonism, but the last part of her question just suddenly jumped into the mind and she blurted it out. She began laughing as the next odd thought also just popped into her head.

"Oh my God Ellen! The witch that lived here turned him into a frog! Ha! Ha! Ha!"
With that Ellen began laughing as well. In their laughter neither of them happened to noticed that the KII was now lit up solid with all six lights. What happen next though snapped both of them out of their laughter and sent a chill up their spines. The child's voice that came from the closet was soft but clear. The tone was obviously one of annoyance.

"There aren't any frogs in here!"

Sarah sat motionless on the floor, her back against the bed, she had not taken her eyes off the dark mass that had come from inside the closet. The shadow figure was now completely exposed and standing beside the closet door. It blocked out a mirror that was hung on the wall beside the closet. Whatever this thing was it was darker than the dark of the room and seemed to be solid. Sarah could tell it was a man by its shape and size. It stood close to six foot tall. She could make out the head, body, arms and legs, but the legs seemed to disappear into the shadows of the floor, they were less distinct than the rest of the figure. Sarah had felt the change in the atmosphere of the room just before the figure emerged from the closet. The air had gotten heavy, oppressive, she had a splitting headache that emanated from the back of her head, for her this was a sign that a spirit was trying to communicate with her. Now that the figure was in full view, Sarah could feel an intense anxiety in the room. Anxiety and confusion. She instinctively knew these were not her thoughts or feelings but those of the spirit. She had experienced this many times along with Jack on investigations. She put those thoughts and feelings aside and continued to ask questions.

"Do you need us to pray for you?"

Again the KII on the floor in front of her flashed, but this time it would not stop. The dark figure now moved closer to Sarah and was standing right in front of the KII meter. Sarah still did not move, she was still frozen in place. She suddenly realized that she could not even move her body if she wanted to. Her heart began to race with this realization. Now she began to panic. It was the crackle of her walkie-talkie and the sound of Jack's voice that snapped her back from the brink.

"Do you realize you're scaring this family!?"

Jack's tone was firm and demanding. He had been watching what was going on with Sarah on the DVR and because Mia's room was located right above the kitchen he could just make out what Sarah was saying. He had been hoping to intervene with the figure and get it to back off by using a firm voice with it. It had the opposite effect. The lights on the KII light up solid and the dark figure moved quickly forward toward Sarah! Sarah froze! She had not expected this type of activity or response, and she was now too frightened to even think straight. Jack saw what was happening and yelled at her over the walkie.

"Sarah move! Get out of there! I'm on my way!"

Again, Jack's voice snapped Sarah back! She dropped the recorder and reached for something in her jacket pocket.

Jack spun from his chair at the table and raced towards the stairway. Beck had heard him yell and came running out of Maria's room.

"What the hell is going on!?"

Jack ignored her question as he made a mad dash around the corner and up the narrow stairs to the second floor. He yelled back to Beck to stay back at basecamp and keep an eye on the TV monitor, keep track of everyone. As he made his way up the stairs he heard a blood curdling scream at that same moment he heard Sharon swearing.

"What the fuck!"

Jack reached the top of the landing to the hallway and was about to head for Mia's bedroom door when he saw a bright flash of white light emanate from Renata's bedroom, followed immediately by a blue light orb and then a red light orb flying out of her doorway and down the hall directly at him! This time Jack froze in place, stunned by what he was witnessing. All he could think was "what the hell...?" This time it was Sarah's voice that snapped Jack back to reality.

"Jack! In here!"

Sarah's voice sounded frightened and urgent. Jack darted to Mia's door and swung it open just as the two light orbs darted past him. He nearly fell into the room.

"Sarah! You okay!"

She was still sitting on the floor against the bed, but she now had a small flashlight held tightly in both hands. It was emitting a purple colored light that she was shining intently on the closet door. He could see Sarah was shaking a bit, as was he, and he could hear a bit of fear in her voice as she spoke.

"Yeah...Yeah I'm okay now. I suddenly remembered I had my UV light with me and used it on the shadow figure. Jack, it actually screamed like it was in pain and darted back into the closet!"

Jack stood slumped over in the doorway, breathing a sigh of relief and trying to catch his breath, or so he thought. "WHUMP!!!" The door to Laceys' room came flying open and hit the door stop. Jack jumped as did Sarah.

"What the hell is going on!?"

Sharon saw Jack slumped in the doorway and yelled more in concern than for any other reason. Jack nearly fell over again.

"What the fuck Sharon! Jesus! You just gave me a second heart attack! Sarah and her shadow figure gave me the first one!"

Sharon looked at him puzzled, Ellen sprang out of Laceys' room right behind Sharon.

"What the heck was that scream!? Oh My God Jack! Sharon and I just heard a child yell at us from Laceys' closet!"

Jack felt stupefied. None of them had ever witnessed that much activity in that short a period of time on any investigation. They had ever done. He looked over at Sarah who was still sitting on the floor hold the flashlight on the closet. He stood up, composed himself and spoke calmly to Sarah as he walked over to her and helped her up.

"Come on Sarah, it's alright now."

Ellen and Sharon looked at them puzzled. They had no idea what had just transpired, but Ellen could see her daughter was a bit shaken up.

"Sarah, what happened?"

Jack made sure Sarah went in front of him as they walked away from the closet. He turned to Ellen and Sharon as they stepped out of the room.

"I think we all need to go back to basecamp with Beck and regroup before we investigate further. We have a lot to discuss and we need to re-access our game plan."

Beck was sitting in front of the TV monitor as the team entered the kitchen. Jack settled in against the kitchen counter near the sink, Ellen sat down at the table next to Beck, Sarah and Sharon sat at the opposite end of the table from Ellen and Beck. Sharon grabbed her can of pop from her cooler bag she had brought and cracked it open. Everyone else followed suit with their own drinks they had brought. Then they began discussing all that had just happened, everyone looked to be a little shell-shocked by it all. Ellen turned to Jack for his opinion of it all.

"Jack, given the experiences we all just had, what do you think we're dealing with here? Is it possibly demonic? Should we pack it up and call in our demonologist and Psychic friends Katie and Beckah Boyd?"

Jack did not like walking away from any case and Ellen knew it, but she also knew if he really thought it could be or was dangerous then he would back off from it and get some additional help. Jack took a moment to consider Ellen's questions before responding.

"Well I do believe we are definitely dealing with a lot of energy in this house, but I'm not ready to call anything here a demon at this point. Yes, we've had some startling and frightening experiences, but no one has been harmed."

Sarah piped up with her own question and a reminder about something Jack himself had told them.

"But what about the entity I chased away with the UV light? You've always told us that negative spirits are harmed by UV light, and I would think the fact that the light made it scream and run means that it is negative."

Jack nodded his agreement with her.

"Yeah, that's right."

Beck chimed in.

"I agree with Sarah. Given what she experienced that thing sure isn't exactly friendly."

Jack leaned forward from the sink and stood up straight. He addressed his response to the entire group.

"Yes, I agree it seems to be a negative entity, but at the same time that doesn't mean it's demonic. Even negative human spirits are affected by UV light. I think if there was something truly demonic here, we would have experienced some other kind of significant violent activity, and we haven't. The fact that we are still standing here talking about it I believe confirms that. Whatever is here knows we are here, and knows why we are here. If it wanted us out, we would already be gone. It would do something to make it very clear to us."

At that exact moment the entire house began to slowly shake. Glasses, pots, pans and dishes began to rattle, the team watched as the TV monitor began to sway side to side on the table, a rumbling sound could be heard within the entire house, and then the entire house began to sway from side to side, then....it all just stopped, and there was dead silence. Ellen glared up at Jack.

"Tell me now it's not demonic!"

Jack rolled his eyes. He hated when people just jumped to conclusions. He was a rational person, perhaps sometimes too rational, but he knew what they had just experienced was not caused by anything demonic. He explained to Ellen what they had just experienced.

"Ellen, it's not a demon causing this, it's a seismic event, a small earth quake. I've experienced many just like this is San Diego and Yuma, Arizona. There must be a fault line up through this area."

A big grin came across Jack's face.

"It is one hell of a coincidence though isn't it."

All of the ladies just glared at him, but it was Sharon that scolded him.

"You know that would almost be funny if the house wasn't shaking apart around us!"

Jack knew they were all concerned, he could see it in their faces, and they had a right to be, but he was always still impressed by this team, because even with all that had just happened, the team was still together in the house, they had not panicked and they had not left. Not yet anyway, and even if they made the decision to go, it would be an agreed to decision and an orderly retreat. Jack felt he could get them to stay though, to finish the investigation and help this family.

He just had no feeling of there being anything demonic about this case. Strange things, yes. Odd coincidences, absolutely. Demonic, no. He addressed them all again.

"The house isn't shaking apart around us. Look, its' already stopped. It was just a minor tremor, that's all."

Ellen expressed everyone's concern.

"But how do we know for sure that's all it was?"

Jack was honest with his reply.

"We don't right now, except for my own experiences with them, but I'll contact the U.S. Geological Survey Office on Monday, and see if they recorded any seismic events in this area at this time and day. In the meantime we need to continue with this investigation and try to find out more of what's going on for the client. With that said though, is everyone okay to continue? We can always still call for a general retreat if anything else negative does happen to anyone. We do this to try and help people right? What good are we doing if we walk away at this point? So who's with me to stay?"

Jack raised his right hand, and looked to around the table to see who else was in agreement.

"This needs to be unanimous, or none of us stay."

Sharon was the first to raise hers.

"Yeah, I'm in."

Then Beck.

"Me too. This is what we do and why we're here right?"

Sarah raised hers.

"Let's go for it."

Ellen was the last holdout. She had her arms crossed and was sitting back in her chair. Beck nudged her with an elbow. Ellen gave her a glance, then grudgingly raised her hand as well.

"Fine. We'll stay. For now, but jack, if this house starts shaking again, we are GONE!"

Jack looked at her and smiled.

"Ellen if this house starts shaking again, I'll be the first one out the door."

He looked at the team around the table.

"Okay! Let's get back upstairs and push these spirits for a few more answers. Sarah you're with me in Laceys' room. Sharon and Ellen hit the basement for a bit then come back upstairs to the second floor bedrooms and check out David's bedroom. Beck, do

you mind staying on the monitor?"
Beck grinned, she actually liked the idea of keeping an eye on everyone this time.

"I'm good with that. No problem."
The rest of the nights' investigation was filled with additional activity that validated the family's claims including more bright flashes of bright white light in both Renata's and Mia's rooms. Responses on the KII and also the Ghost Radar application that Jack uses on his smart phone. The device allows spirits to communicate through words and energy blips on the application. Knocking and dragging sounds were heard in the attic where Sarah and Sharon investigated, but could not find a source of the noises. Around 11:55 am Jack switched out with Beck at the monitor so she could investigate with Ellen. Beck, like Jack and Sarah, was sensitive to spirits and usually got a lot of activity around her during investigations. Beck joined Ellen in David's room.

"Is the little boy here? Can you give us a sign that you're here?"
Beck's question was followed by a loud screeching sound as the KII meter near the closet light up. Beck's eyes got wide and she swore in surprise.

"What the fuck was that?!"
Ellen jumped at the screeching sound

"I don't know! Quick play it back on the recorder!"
They both leaned in to listen to the play back.

Jack watched each of the rooms on the monitor closely, and kept an eye on his team members. He looked at time on the monitor, it was 2:04 am. He picked up his walkie off the table.

"Okay, everyone, it's after 2:00 am, let's wrap it up and break it all down. Time to go home."

Two weeks later the S.P.I.R.I.T.S. team was gathered in their office to go over the evidence from the Rodriguez family investigation. Jack and Sharon were seated at the head of the conference table with the large TV monitor behind them which was hooked up to a laptop computer. Ellen sat at the opposite end of the table with Beck to her right and Sarah to her left. They all settled in and Jack began.

"Okay, what do you want first, the good news or the bad news?"
Ellen looked at him and mused.

"How bad is the bad news?"

Jack rubbed the back of his neck. He knew what he was about to tell Ellen was not going to go over well.

"Well, you know the shadow figure that seemed to go after Sarah, and how it was right in line with the IR camera we had setup?

Ellen nodded as she drew out her response.

"Yeaahhh…."

Jack's face cringed as he dreaded the reaction to what he was about to tell her.

"Well, we had a little accident, an incident you could say, during the review, and we lost that section of the footage."

Jack held his breath as he waited for the reaction from the three at the end of the table. Ellen's reaction was worse than he thought it would be. Ellen pounded her fist on the table and screamed.

"WHAT! AND WHO'S RESPONSIBLE FOR THAT!"

Ellen's question was a rhetorical one, as she knew full well who was responsible for reviewing the DVR evidence, but she wanted to make her displeasure with the incident completely clear. Jack responded back calmly. He could see that Beck and Sarah we also taken aback by Ellen's reaction.

"Ellen, I understand you're upset, but it really doesn't matter who was reviewing the evidence when it happened, the fact is it was an accident, it could have happened to any of us. Hell, we've all screwed up at one time or anoth…"

Because he was sitting right beside Sharon, Jack did not see that Sharon was getting angry herself, and was upset by Ellen's reaction to the news and her question as to whose fault it was. He had totally focused on Ellen when Sharon cut him off.

"No one needs to defend me! I can do that for myself! Yeah, I screwed up Ellen! In reviewing the DVR I forgot to make a copy of that section of the footage before reviewing more of it! I also didn't check to see how much space was left on the DVR when I started so the system overwrote some of the footage to make space for other clips I was saving! It's my fault! I fucked up! So if you want I'll quit the team and you won't have to worry about it ever again! Yeah I screwed up! Don't you think I feel bad enough about it without you screaming at me as if you were my mother! Well you're not!"

Jack just sat there in silence, he dare not say another word at this point. Sharon had made it clear that this was between her and Ellen and no one else. Sarah and Beck also fell silent. Ellen sat there for a moment, not saying anything. She realized she had stepped over the line and over-reacted to the loss of the evidence. Her mind set had just been about the loss of that validation of the shadow figure to the family. It upset her deeply, but she knew she had no right to react the way she did. Sharon worked hard on every case to review the hours and hours of DVR footage and a lot of the audio as well. Ellen calmed herself and spoke in a sincere tone.

"Sharon, I'm sorry. I had no right to react like that. You and Jack both work very hard at reviewing all of the hours and hours of audio and video so we can get answers for our clients. I'm sorry. No one wants you to quit."

Sharon was still angry, her face showed it, but she could tell Ellen was being sincere in her apology.

"Well next time ask what happened before you jump down our throats! You're right, we do work hard at this, and sometimes we are going to make mistakes, but I did screw up and it was important evidence and now it's gone. Maybe I shouldn't be on this team anymore. That was a serious screw up on my part."

Jack felt the tension ebb. He leaned forward and put his hand on Sharon's shoulder.

"No one is quitting. You can't quit your family. Look, we still have a lot of great evidence and some answers to give Maria and her family, and that's more important than any 30 seconds of footage that doesn't account for much when getting answers for this family is our goal."

Beck reached out and took Ellen's hand.

"Agreed! Well said Jack. Now can we put this BS behind us and finish going over the evidence please?"

The team spent the next three hours going over all of the EVPs and video evidence to determine what was relevant and worthy of presenting to the client, as well as coming to a consensus of what the evidence meant and if there was any real danger to the family from the activity.

Three weeks to the day of the investigation, the S.P.I.R.I.T.S. of New England team returned to the Rodriguez home to go over their findings with the family, and discuss what actions to take next to resolve the paranormal issues. Everyone had gathered in the living to go over all of the evidence. Jack sat on the floor in front of the coffee table. His laptop was setup at the far end of it so everyone could see the screen on it. He also plugged a small portable high quality speaker system into the laptop so everyone could hear the EVPs better, instead of just using the speakers built into the laptop. After going through several EVPs and some of the video evidence Jack gave the family a breakdown of it all and what the team believed was in the home.

"So from what you just saw and heard, our team has come to the conclusion that you have at least two spirits in your home. One child and one adult male. There is something else going on here as well, something non-paranormal that is likely fueling the activity."

Jack pulled up a new file on the computer, containing information he had obtained from the U.S.G.S.

"You may find this hard to believe but the bed shaking you are experiencing is actually being caused by seismic activity that regularly occurs in this area."

Maria was more than surprised by the information.

"You mean we have earth quakes here!"

Jack gave her a soft smile of reassurance.

"Yes, exactly, but please don't worry. I spoke to the U.S. Geological Survey local office and although there is a fault line that runs along the Merrimack River, the tremors that emanate from it are small, 0.1 to 0.3 on the Richter scale. The only reason you feel them here is because your house foundation sits on the granite bedrock up here on the hills above the river, so the bedrock acts as an amplifier of the shock waves from the tremors."

Jack looked around at the family, again with a smile, and again to reassure them about what he was going to tell them next. It was important that they know he and the team had a handle on all of this and were going to be able to help them, and give them some real answers.

"The seismic activity is also what is generating the strange lights you see in the house. What they are is a release of energy from within the earth just prior to a seismic event. Those are the lights you see in the footage from one of our DVR cameras. Unfortunately, this energy can also provide fuel for spirits to feed on and increase their strength and their ability to interact with our world."

Maria still look a bit concerned, and she still had questions for the team.

"So what can we do? I don't want these spirits bothering poor Lacey and the rest of my family anymore, so how do we stop it?"

Ellen spoke up. She knew Maria and her family were still anxious about all of this, even if they now at least felt validated that they were experiencing a haunting.

"First I want to assure you that we don't believe either of these spirits is trying to harm anyone. The male figure seems to be desperate to make contact, but we don't believe he's out to harm anyone. The child just seems to want to make friends with Lacey. I want you to listen to this one EVP again we captured in Lacys' room. It's of this child's voice."

Everyone crowded in around the small coffee table to listen to the EVP again. The volume was turned up so everyone jumped a bit when the audio started. This is what they heard....

Ellen: Are you the boy that talks to Lacey?

Sharon: Lacey says you're an ugly green boy. Why are you green? Are you a frog? Oh my God Ellen! The witch that lived here turned him into a frog!

Both: Ha! Ha! Ha! Ha! Ha! Ha!

Child Spirit: There aren't any frogs in here!

The voice was clear and obvious. Jack played it twice more and then discussed it with the family.

"So as you heard, it's a young child's voice responding to Sharon and letting her know there are no frogs in the closet. So again, there is nothing negative here. They are not trying to hurt anyone, just make contact."

Maria seemed a little more at ease, but still had more questions.

"Okay, I do feel a little better about that part, but they still are scary to Lacey and we do want them to leave us alone so what do we do next?"

Ellen knew exactly what they all needed to do next as did the rest of the team. Ellen looked directly into Maria's eyes as she spoke, so Maria would understand the importance of what she was about to tell her.

"What we do next is we go upstairs with all of you and speak out loud to these spirits and make it clear their interaction with you is not wanted, and has to stop immediately. We will also go through your home and check for, and close, any spirit portals that might be here. While we do that we will make it clear to the male spirit that he needs to move on and cannot stay here any longer. He needs to cross over to the other side."

Jack added to Ellen's statement.

"I will also do a house cleansing using white sage to clear the home of any spirits and any negative energy in the home.

Maria looked at Jack a bit puzzled.

"What is white sage?"

Jack explained.

"White sage is a kind of incense that is used to cleanse a home or even a person of any negative energy. Think of it as stain remover, but for your home and your spirit."

Maria and her family laughed.

"Okay, got it. What happens after all that? Is there anything else we need to do?"

Ellen interjected again.

"After that it's a bit of a waiting game to see if activity dies down over the next few weeks. During that time, I want you to re-sage the house once every week. Jack will show you how to do that and we will leave the white sage with you. Also, keep letting any spirits that might still be here know that they need to keep to themselves or they have to leave. It's your home now, not theirs, they need to respect that, and your family."

Maria still looked a bit skeptical and still had concerns.

"And if that doesn't work? Then what?"

This time it was Jack that looked straight into Maria's eyes as he spoke, but he kept that reassuring smile of his.

"Maria, it will work. It always does. Sometimes it takes a while, and it can take more than one house cleansing to accomplish. We also have other things we can do, and we have some friends of ours we can get to assist us if necessary. Remember, just because we are finishing up the investigation with you today does not mean we are going away completely. We will be here for you whenever you need us. We NEVER just walk away from people that need our help."

"Then saith Jesus unto him, Get thee hence, Satan: for it is written, Thou shalt worship the Lord thy God, and him only shalt thou serve."

Matthew 4:10 - King James Version (KJV)

MERRIMAC PAPER CO.

4
THE WHEEL
AND
THE WELL

*Six days shall work be done, but on the seventh day there shall be to
you an holy day, a sabbath of rest to the LORD: whosoever doeth
work therein shall be put to death.*
Exodus 35:2 – King James Version (KJV)

This was going to be a different investigation for the S.P.I.R.I.T.S.
team for two big reasons; One, they had never investigated an old
factory before, the place was massive! To be honest it was a bit
overwhelming, and two, the team was down two investigators. Jack
was home sick with the flu, and Beck was away visiting her mother
down in Georgia, so for this one it was left to Ellen, Sharon and
Sarah to handle.

The old Merrimac Paper Mill stood looming before the three
ladies. Even in its current state of decay it was still an impressive site.
It opened its doors for business in 1886 on the South Canal of the
Merrimac River in Lawrence, Massachusetts. It remained a working
paper mill until it was sold in 2005. After that the building began to
degrade, being bought and sold a few times until it was purchased by
its most recent owner, Mr. Daniel Patrick. His paranormal problems
with the building started shortly after he began renovations on the
old paper mill. When workers began gutting the place two months
earlier they started seeing shadow figures moving through the
abandoned hallways, hearing disembodied conversations, and
someone walking on the third floor office areas when no one else
was up there. When coming to work in the morning they would find
tools missing, or moved to another part of the building with no
explanation. There was security on duty at night and no work was
going on in the building from 8:00 pm until 7:00 am each day. Over
the last couple of weeks activity seemed to ramp up while working in
the basement area of the building. Workers were hearing the voice
and scream of a woman, and some workers were even being touched
and scratched by something they could not see. Some of the workers
began walking off the job because of the activity. It was at that point
that Daniel contacted the S.P.I.R.I.T.S. of New England team for
help.

So now here they were, waiting outside this monster of a building
in the rain for the owner to come and let them in, and give them a
quick tour before they got to work investigating. They did not have
to wait long though before Daniel and his security officer for the

building pulled up in his black SUV.

Daniel stepped out of the SUV. He had a big smile on his face.
  "Hello ladies! How are you doing this evening?"
It was just about 7:00 pm on a Saturday, and since it was now fall the sun was beginning to set. The Shadow of the decrepit building stretched over them, and the air had begun to grow cold. Ellen smiled back and reached out her hand to greet him.
  "We're all doing good Dan, thank you. Jack sends his apologizes for not being here tonight, he was just too sick to make it."
Dan gave her a firm hand shake.
  "No problem Ellen. Jack called me this morning and let me know he wasn't going to be able to make it. I know I'm in good hands with all of you ladies though."
Sharon quipped back at him and laughed.
  "You don't know us too well then do you!"
Dan laughed.
  "No but I have a feeling I'm about to find out."

Dan and the security guard lead the team to a side entrance of the building where they enter through a steel security door. Currently this was only one of two access doors into the building, everything else was boarded up to prevent anyone from entering who did not have permission to be there. Dan had a good reason for keeping the place locked up tight, and Ellen and the team were about to find that out.
  The sun was now low in the sky as the security guard opened the door to let everyone enter. Sharon stepped in first followed by Sarah, then Ellen, and then Dan. The guard attached a wire connected to the wall to the door handle to hold it open and let some light in. The building was completely dark inside, except for a few rays of now diminishing sunlight that squeezed their way through some of the small cracks and holes in the boards covering up the windows. The little bit of light was just enough to allow them to see all of the debris that was scattered about the floor from the construction that was going on. Old factory equipment, office furniture, and papers littered the open shop floor they had just walked into. They could also see the dust floating in the air as it passed through the rays of sunlight. It was certainly an eerie atmosphere. It gave one the impression of a tomb, or what the world might be like after an apocalyptic event,

either way it was an obviously a dangerous place.

Sharon took out her flashlight and began scanning the room, she noticed that on the floor, about fifteen feet in front from them, there was a very dark spot that her flashlight could not illuminate. She began to walk towards it when Dan spoke up.

"Be careful Sharon, that's just a big hole in the floor where one of the old boilers for the mill used to be. It's about a twenty foot drop to the basement below. There are three openings in the floor just like that one."

Sharon stopped and looked back at him in astonishment.

"Are you serious?! Wholly crap! You just leave them open like that?!"

Dan was slightly taken aback by her response. Ellen stood there for a moment feeling a bit mortified. Dan explained the situation to Sharon.

"Well yes. We have to leave them open for now because we are still in the processes of deconstructing those pits and the boilers that were in them. That's part of the reason why we keep this placed sealed up tight so no one can get in. We don't want anyone wandering in off the streets and falling into one of those holes, or falling off the old catwalk 20 feet above your head."

Sharon pointed her flashlight up at the ceiling thirty-feet above them, she panned it around until she caught the catwalk in her beam. It looked old and a bit rusted, but it was a place she immediately thought she had to check out. She looked back over to Dan.

"So is that catwalk safe to walk on?"

Dan smiled and laughed.

"Oh so the big holes in the floor aren't a problem anymore?

Sharon smiled back.

"Not as long as I can check out that catwalk!"

Dan nodded.

"Yes, it's safe. But you still need to be careful up there. You might want to do one of your EVP sessions up there as a couple of my guys did report seeing and hearing someone walking up there, but they know they were alone in the building at the time and the person just seemed to disappear in the middle of the catwalk. There is also a story about one of the mill workers falling to his death from there. He was supposedly offered overtime to come in on a Sunday and paint the catwalk. I don't know how true that is, but I do know there were many accidents in here, and there are a couple of documented deaths from workers getting caught in the machines. There is also a story of a woman being murdered by her husband down in the basement section. As it was told to me the wife thought her husband was cheating on her during the night shift with another woman that worked here. The wife came here to check on him one night, and caught him in the basement office with the other woman. The woman took off and the husband was furious. He grabbed his wife and tossed her head first into the big flywheel that's down there, killing her. He then called the police but he told them it was an accident, and that in a fit of anger she ran up the stairs, lost her footing, and fell into it the flywheel. The police couldn't prove otherwise so the husband was never arrested.

The guys working for me believe it's the woman that was murdered that they hear talking and screaming down there. They also believe the reason some of them have been touched and scratched is because she hates men, and is still trying to take out her anger for her husband on them. They also reported to me the faint smell of a woman's perfume near the well down there. It's not the kind of well you might think, it was used to gain access to the river that runs under that section of the building. They used the river to power generators in the Paper Mill in the early to middle 1900's."

The three ladies stood there in awe listening to everything Dan was telling them. If even half of it were true, it was going to be a good investigation. Sarah spoke first.

"Wow, that's some crazy stuff."

Ellen always took stories like that to heart. A woman being abused, let alone murdered by her husband, was just repugnant to her.

"That's awful! I can't believe he could get away with killing his own wife! That bastard!"

Sharon turned to her.

"Well it's only a story Ellen, they don't know for sure if it's true or not. We will definitely do an EVP session down there to try and find out though."

The group spent the next hour and half touring through the building and also into a second connected building where the workers had also experienced seeing shadow figures, hearing voices and footsteps. They regrouped back at the side entrance door where they had come in.

"Well ladies that's everything. I have to get going but Bob here will be around all night if you need him. Just keep this walkie with you and call him when you need him to let you out of the building. There is one working bathroom just down to your left here if you need to use it. There are also a couple working electrical outlets along this main wall here so feel free to use them, but that is the only electricity in the building right now. Bob will help you carry in anything you need from your cars and then he has to lock you in for the evening. Again, be careful in here, but also have fun and try to figure out what's really going on for me okay. Many of my guys are ready to just walk off the job due to all of the activity. It's a real problem for me."

The ladies all smiled at him. Ellen shook his hand again.

"Thank you Dan, and don't worry we will get you some answers, we promise."

They all walked out to the cars together. Bob helped the women carry their equipment into the building and then locked them in.

The team needed to set up basecamp to have a place to organize from and get the DVR system up and running. They found an old metal office desk against the main wall not far from the bathroom. Sarah and Sharon dragged it back towards the entrance door near one of the working outlets. They would use it as basecamp and to setup the DVR system on, not that anyone would sit to monitor it this time, they would stay together during the whole investigation due to their lack of numbers and the real potential physical dangers within the place.

They had four cameras to use. They setup one right in the main shop area not far from the door, looking up at the catwalk where the apparition had been seen. The second one they setup in the basement looking up the stairwell and at the big flywheel where the woman had supposedly been murdered. The third they setup looking down the basement hallway toward the well as shadow figures had been reported there as also. The last one they setup on the third floor in the old office area where shadow figures had been seen, as well as people talking and footsteps had been heard. A digital voice recorder was also setup in the same area with each camera, as well as what is called a Ghost Meter, which is another type of EMF meter, but has a red light that flashes and an audible alarm that sounds when it detects any energy. They set these up in view of each DVR camera. Sharon had gone up and placed one in the middle of the catwalk which almost gave Ellen a heart attack watching her up there.

After securing the last camera on the third floor they regrouped back at basecamp. Each of them grabbed an additional audio recorder, and a handheld IR video camera. Sarah took a KII meter and Sharon grabbed a Mel-Meter. Ellen setup her Ghost Radar App on her phone, being sure to set the phone in airplane mode first before starting the application. They were now ready to roll on the investigation. Ellen looked to Sharon.

"Where do you want to start first?"
Sharon did not hesitate to answer, as she looked up.

"I really want to start up on that catwalk…"
She did not get to finish her thought when she saw something move along the walk and then the Ghost Meter sounded off. BEEP! BEEP! BEEP! All of them were stunned!

"What the hell!"
That was about all Sharon could bring herself to say. She looked at Sarah and Ellen.

"We have got to go up there and now!"
Sarah shot back.

"I totally agree!"
Ellen was not so eager.

"No, we can observe it and ask questions right from here where it's safer!

Both Sarah and Sharon glared at her. Sarah was in disbelief.

"Mom. Seriously are you kidding? This is what we're here for! You know Jack would go up there if he were here, or he would at least send two of us up there!"
Ellen scowled at her daughter.

"Well Jack's not here and you're not going up there, and neither am I!"
Sarah knew even Jack would agree with that statement. If he was not there to call the shots it was up to Ellen and Sharon to decide what to do.

"That's fine. I'll go up and you two stay here and keep an eye on me."

Sharon was quick to make a command decision. She knew someone had to go up there. She could not send Sarah and Ellen was not going to let her go anyway, but Sharon could choose to go herself. It was her own risk to take if she wanted to, and she had already been up there once and knew the platform was sound, and knew how to get up there. Yes, the building way dark but they all had flashlights and their phones they could use as flashlights if they needed to. She turned to Sarah and Ellen.

"Do me a favor and give me more light by holding your flashlights on me as I go up there, don't blind me with them but shine them towards my feet so I can see better where I'm going."

Ellen was still concerned.

"Okay but be careful! I really don't like this."

Sharon gave her a wave and headed towards the metal stairway along the far wall that lead up to the catwalk. Ellen and Sarah provided her with the light she had asked for.

The shadow figure had been there and gone the minute Sharon looked up at it. For a moment she was not even sure if she had really seen it, until the Ghost Meter went off as well. She had to get up there to find out what was going on. Was it really a shadow figure she had seen or a trick of lights and shadows? What had really made the meter light up and alarm? Was it something paranormal or something with a more natural explanation? She need to find out, not only for their client but for herself, and she knew it would gnaw at her until she did.

With the help of the extra lighting from Ellen and Sarah it only took her a few minutes to reach the top of the stairs and the platform to the catwalk. She stood there for a moment just looking across the catwalk to the far side where there was just another stairway leading back down to the main floor. She could have taken that one but the one she chose to use was closer to the basecamp setup. She turned on her handheld IR camera and the IR light for it, and used the viewer on the camera to look across the catwalk. The infrared spectrum of the camera allowed her to see in the dark like an animal. It also allowed her to see in a spectrum of light that humans cannot normally see in. She was hoping it might reveal something hiding in the shadows that she could not see with her own eyes. The catwalk, platform, and stairways were empty. She slowly moved toward the center of the catwalk where she had placed the Ghost Meter earlier. She took two steps forward on the walk, the meter quickly beeped and flashed twice.

"BEEP! BEEP!"

Sharon froze. Ellen and Sarah had been watching her from the ground still providing the extra light she asked for. They both saw and heard the meter go off. Sarah called up to her.

"Sharon, do you think stepping onto the catwalk made it go off?"

It was not a bad first guess at what might have happened, given that the meter went off twice after Sharon took two steps onto the walk. Without taking her eyes off the meter, Sharon spoke in a low tone back to Sarah. If something was up there with her she did not want to disturb it by yelling.

"It's possible I suppose, but I didn't set it off when I first left it up here. I'll take another step."

She slowly took one more step toward the device. It went off again.

"BEEP!"

Sharon stood there puzzled. This should not be happening. The meter is not motion sensitive, it is only affected by electro-magnetic frequency, radio signal, or even a cell phone signal. She reached into her coat pocket. Nope, no cell phone. She knew she had turned it off and left it on the table with the DVR system as did Sarah. The only person with a cell phone was Ellen and she had hers in airplane mode to run the Ghost Radar App. She did have her walkie on her though. She reached to her side, unclipped it from her belt, and clicked the talk button. The only thing that happened was the one Sarah had on her made that typical weird tweeting sound, but the meter remained silent.

Ellen was pensively watching her. She did not like Sharon being up there.

"Okay Sharon, I think it's just you causing it to go off. Why don't you just come back down. Whatever happened before is over, and we will have caught it on camera and audio anyway."

Sharon was a bit annoyed with Ellen. She knew Ellen was just worried about her, but they were there to investigate and she was not coming down until she figured this out. She kept her composure and spoke calmly back to Ellen.

"Ellen. I really don't think it's me. It doesn't make sense. I'm going to…"

She did not get to finish. The meter suddenly began beeping and flashing like crazy, then it just suddenly slid across the catwalk and off the edge. It fell twenty-feet and smashed onto the concrete floor below. A deep cold chill ran up Sharon's spine. At that exact moment the device fell from the catwalk she swore she heard a man screaming. Whatever composure she had been maintaining went over the edge with the device. She yelled down to her two friends.

"Jesus! Did you guys hear that! Did you hear a man scream?!"

Sarah was quick with her response.

"Yeah, I heard that too!"

Ellen was just freaked out; she did not care about any voice anyone heard. Her first concern was for Sharon.

"Sharon! That's it! Get down here now! Before you end up smashed on that floor like that meter!"

Sharon really wanted to keep investigating the catwalk, but with the meter broken on the floor, and the way it slid on its own and off the walk, she felt Ellen was probably right this time. The best course of action was to just step back and give whatever was there some space. She was also getting that feeling like she should not be there, and the feeling was intensifying. She knew it was time to head back down.

"Yeah I think you're right Ellen."

She backed off from the catwalk and headed back down the stairway. Ellen felt much better once Sharon stepped off the stairs onto the floor.

Sarah walked over and picked up the meter from the ground. It was cracked and broken, the nine-volt battery was hanging out of the back of it. Just for the heck of it she pressed the power button. Nothing happened. She stated the obvious to the others.

"Yep, it's broken."

She carried it back to the desk and placed the broken device on it. Her mother looked at her.

"What did you bring that back for? It's no good."

Sarah shrugged.

"Maybe Jack can fix it. Besides we shouldn't leave are junk laying around."

Ellen looked around the place and then back at Sarah.

"Are you serious? Do you really think they would notice?"

Sarah gave her mother a look.

"It doesn't matter if they notice or not, we will know. I'm not

65

leaving trash in here, regardless of how much is already on the
floor. It's not about the trash, it's about our reputation."
Sharon nodded her agreement.

"Yeah, that's true."
Ellen capitulated.

"You're right dear. I hadn't really thought of it that way."

The women took a few minutes to discuss the activity they had just
experienced. It was hard to believe an hour and forty-five had already
passed and they had not even left the basecamp area yet. It was now
9:20 pm. They found it interesting that what they experienced on the
catwalk seemed to confirm the story of a man falling to his death
from it. It would take review of the audio and video to see what more
they may have captured, as well as some serious research to see if
there was any truth to the story. They needed to move on though,
and investigate the other locations they had planned. Ellen again
deferred to Sharon as to where to go next.

"Well we can go to any of the three other spots. What do you
think Sarah?"
Sarah knew exactly where she wanted to go next.

"Let's head down to the basement and the flywheel where the
woman was supposed to have been murdered. I also want to see if
we can debunk the smell of perfume down by the well."
Sharon agreed.

"Good idea. Let's go."
The three women grabbed their gear and headed down to the
basement.

The stairwell into the basement was pitch black, there were no
windows down there for any ambient light to get in. Sarah was first in
line. She took a moment at the top of the stairs to stare into the
darkness below. Nothing. She could see absolutely nothing but the
blackness. Even the stairs just disappeared less than halfway in front
of her into it, as if they just ended. It was then she felt a cold chill run
through her. She could sense something was not right. Something
was down there, something she could not see, something that was
staring back at her, something that somehow knew she was standing
at the top of the stairs. It frightened her, but only for a moment, the
single moment it took to hesitate at the stop of the stairs and peer

into the apparent abyss below. Then it came to her. A single memory of a quote from her favorite television show, and her favorite Doctor; "Do what I do. Hold tight and pretend it's a plan!" She pointed her flashlight down the stairwell, it illuminated her way. The stairs did not end in nothingness, and she could see the bottom ten feet below. The feeling of being watched remained though.

"Is everything okay Sarah?"

Sharon's voice startled her, and snapped her back from her thoughts.

"Oh, yeah. Sorry. I'm just getting that sense of being watched. Anyway, let's head down."

The three ladies walked slowly down the stairwell into the blackness. About halfway down they came across the large flywheel where the woman had supposedly been murdered by her husband. They stopped and looked it over. It was intimidating for sure, and completely capable of killing someone. It was about five feet in circumference, made of forged steel, and the six wheel spokes were about six to eight inches in diameter. If someone was tossed head first into that when it was turning at 1200 rpms, as indicated on the sign next to it, they would not survive it. They would be decapitated. Although the death would be instant for sure, it would be brutal and very bloody. If a woman really was murdered that way in that wheel, it would have been so quick that she might not even know she was dead, at least that was the thought that crossed Ellen's mind as she looked the thing over.

"Do you both think someone was really murdered down here with that thing?"

Both Sharon and Sarah looked back at her, and responded almost in unison.

"I don't know."

The two of them looked at each other, but Sarah got it out first.

"Jinx!"

At that moment there was a loud clank sound that came from the darkness further into the basement. All three women turned their flashlights toward the direction of the noise. There was another bang like the sound of an empty trash can falling over, followed by a shuffling sound. It was then that Sharon caught the sight of something moving across the floor down the hallway to the well. It seemed to almost waddle as it moved, then she caught the shine of its eyes in her light, Sarah and Ellen trained their lights onto it as well. It was a rat! Not surprising, Sharon thought, given the place is right on the river.

"Jesus, that thing scared the hell out of me! For a moment I thought it might be some kind of shadow create or something. Ha! Ha!"

Ellen was not as amused.

"You mean to tell me there are rats down here?! That's just great!"

Sarah just shrugged her shoulders and laughed.

"What did you expect? It's an old abandoned factory on the river!"

Ellen shook her head.

"Yeah well you would think…."

She never got to finish her thought, she was interrupted by what sounded like a woman screaming. They were now all at the bottom of the stairs and the sound came from behind them. They all turned back to look. For a moment it seemed like there was nothing happening, then Sarah caught the final movement of the heavy flywheel as it stopped turning. Sharon saw it too.

"What the fuck?!"

Sarah was in dis-belief.

"Sharon, did that flywheel really just move?!"

Ellen was confused.

"What?! The wheel moved?! I heard a woman scream!"

Sharon and Sarah both shook their heads in dis-agreement. Sharon responded to Ellen.

"No, that wasn't a scream. It was that rusted old wheel turning on its own! Sarah and I both saw it!"

Sarah and Sharon walked back up the stairs to the wheel. They reached over the railing and tried to turn it. It took some force but they got it to move a few inches and it made the exact same sound they had just heard, a screeching, squeaking sound, almost like a high pitched scream. The question still remained though, how did it turn on its own in the first place? No one was near it. It took both women to get it to turn, so there was no way any rat or other animal caused it to happen. Sharon and Sarah went back down the stairs to re-join Ellen. Sharon provided her assessment of what they had just witnessed.

"Well whatever caused it to move, it took a lot of energy and force to do it. No rat did it that's for sure. Even we had a hard time moving it, didn't we Sarah?"

They were all staring up at the flywheel, hoping to maybe see it move again. Sarah did not turn her gaze from when she responded.

"Yeah, it was hard to turn for sure. The whole thing is a rusted mess."

Ellen put her hand on her daughters' shoulder.

"Well I just wish I had seen it move myself. That would have been cool. As for what made it move, you know what Jack would say."

Ellen puffed her chest in an attempt to look manly and spoke in a deeper tone of voice.

"Well if you can't find a *normal* cause for it, that just means whatever caused it was *above the normal*; or as we say, it's *paranormal*."

They all laughed. That would be something Jack would say. He was such a jerk that way sometimes. He often loved to state the obvious, and they loved to pick on him for it. Sarah brought the group back to focus.

"Well, while that was interesting, and almost heart stopping, I think we should move on to the well area. I still want to see if we can figure out what is causing the perfume smell they report down that way."

Sharon agreed, but Ellen was not finished with the stairwell yet.

"You two go ahead. I want to spend a little more time here, and try an EVP session. See if I get anything."

Sharon looked at her in disbelief.

"You want to stay here all by yourself? In the dark. With the rat running around."

Ellen walked up the stairs and sat down on them near the old flywheel. She put her flashlight in her pocket, and took out her digital recorder. She set her mini-DV camera down on a stair above her so it could see her and the flywheel. She started her audio recorder.

"Yeah, why not? I mean I'm going to be right here and you and Sarah are only going to be less than forty yards away by the well right? Shouting distance?"

Sharon cocked her head and gave Ellen and odd look.

"Yeah, I suppose."

Sarah piped in.

"Don't argue with her, just let her do her thing. Okay mom, we'll be right down by the well if you need us. Breaking us up might help stir up even more activity anyway, or if a woman was murdered here, she may be more willing to interact with one person rather than several. With most of the reports from down here the person was either alone or there was only two of them."

Sharon found herself unable to really argue with the logic of that given the reports. Maybe Ellen being alone would help get them more answers.

"Okay Ellen, just be careful and use the walkie that Dan gave you to contact the security guard if you need to."

Ellen nodded.

"I will, don't worry. Go check out that well and the perfume smell."

The two women turned and headed down the dark hallway to the well. Ellen sat and began her EVP session.

"Hello, my name is Ellen. I'm here to talk with you. I have a device here in my hand that you can speak into and it will capture your voice. Can you tell me your name?"

It did not take long for Sarah and Sharon to reach the well. Within just a few moments of lingering in the area they caught the fait whiff of a woman's perfume. Sharon sniffed at the air almost like a blood hound.

"Do you smell that? Where is it coming from?"

Sarah did the same, walking in a small circle as she did so. She first held her head up high, then down towards the floor. It was stronger closer to the floor.

"I think it's coming from down in this hole in the floor."

At her feet was a round hole about eight to ten inches in diameter. She shined her flashlight down into it. It seemed to be a small access hole down to some pipes below the floor that lead towards the larger well. Her light caught the glint of something reflective in the bottom of the hole, just below the pipes, it looked to be something made of glass.

"Sharon come here. Take a look at this."

Sharon walked over to Sarah and both women knelt down on the floor over the hole. Sharon shined her light down into it as well. The two flashlights illuminated a small light blue bottle, with a spray top on it. Perfume!

"Damn if that's not a perfume bottle!"

Sharon laid on her side and reached down into the hole. She was just able to get a grip on the bottle with her fingers and pulled it up out of the hole. The bottle was broken on the bottom and the scent of the perfume was strong that emanated from it. Sarah mused at the revelation, and took a moment to celebrate their awesome debunking skills. She smiled from ear to ear.

"Well there's the culprit! Mystery solved Scooby!"
Sharon laughed.

"Ha! Ha! Yeah that didn't take long did it. Are we really that good or just that lucky?"

There was a sudden loud bang that startled them. It made them look up from the bottle and down toward the well. They both saw and heard the Ghosts Meter they had setup on the wall of the well flash and beep several times. It stopped for just a moment and then it started up again. It was then that Sarah felt like she was going to be ill and Sharon spotted the large shadow figure moving back and forth in front of the well and the Ghost Meter. At times it seemed to block out the flashing red light of the meter completely.

The sick feeling came over Sarah suddenly, as soon as the shadow figure had appeared to them.

"Sharon I don't think that thing is friendly at all. I feel sick to my stomach, and I sense a lot of anxiety, and even anger from it."

Sarah was still kneeling on the floor, Sharon had already stood up, and was just staring at the shadow figure that was pacing back and forth not ten feet from them. It was both shocking and mesmerizing to watch. She did not respond to Sarah.

"Sharon! We need to get away from that thing! Help me up!"

Sarah's plea broke Sharon from her trance, but even as she responded to Sarah she did not turn her gaze from the figure before her. In all honesty she was almost afraid to.

"God, I'm sorry Sarah, here take my hand."

She reached her hand out to Sarah and felt her take it. She was a bit taken aback by how cold and even clammy Sarah's hand felt. Maybe her friend was sicker than she had thought. She turned to look at Sarah. Sarah was already standing, and was about four feet away from her. Sharon began to go cold, and felt weak, she felt a wave of energy rush up through her whole body. She could still feel someone gripping her hand tightly, but there was no one there. She spoke softly, her voice was shaking.

"S...S...Sarah?"

Ellen sat alone on the stairwell, it was so quiet in the building that she could hear Sarah and Sharon talking about the hole in the floor and finding the perfume bottle. She thought to herself what a great team they now have. How professional and what great debunkers they are, and how far they had come from their early days as a team. She was proud of her team and of their accomplishments. They had come a long way, and built a strong reputation for themselves. She looked down at the small audio recorder in her hand, it was still on and capturing everything it could hear. She spoke into it to tag the voices of Sarah and Sharon.

"The voices you hear in the background are just Sarah and Sharon down the hallway."

They were taught early on that tagging your audio was one of the most important things you need to do, in order to ensure you did not mistake something you heard as a possible EVP. Making sure everyone on the team reviewed potential EVP's was just as important for that same reason. You did not want to declare something was an EVP if it happened to be one of your team members whispering but they had forgotten to tag it, and you also wanted to gather a consensus as to what class of EVP it was, and what was being said.

Ellen looked down at the recorder again, and thought for a moment. She decided to try an EVP burst session, where you record for a few minutes, asking only a few questions, and then listen back to it for any possible answers from a spirit. She pressed stop on the recorder, then took a moment to explain to whatever spirit might be there what she was about to do, and how they could use the device in her hand to talk to her. She also took out her cell phone that was running the Ghost Radar app and placed it on the stair near the flywheel. The app had been running for a bit now. It was quiet the whole time, it had not spoken any words and no energy blips had appeared on it. Ellen also explained that device to whomever might be listening, and how they could interact with it. She pressed the record button and began to ask her questions, leaving a few seconds in between for any potential response.

"Hello my name is Ellen. Can you please tell me your name?"

"Did you work in this paper mill?"

"Did something happen to you here?"

"Were you injured by this large wheel?"

"Do you need help?"

Ellen stopped the recorder and played it back. She listened for any possible responses. There was nothing. She tried again, but this time took a different approach based on what she thought she was feeling. Jack had told her, if you do not seem to be getting any interaction by asking the typical questions, go with what your gut tells you to ask. Be polite, be considerate, but ask the tough questions if that is what you feel you should do. Sometimes those feelings can come from spirit and those are what they want to talk about with you. It can be what is important to them. She turned the recorder back on.

"So again I am Ellen. I think there is something you want to tell me. I want to hear about what is important to you. Please talk with me."

Just then she noticed a bright red blip grow on the Ghost Radar App. She knew the color red meant it was a source of high energy.

"Oh, so you are here. I can see you on this device. There is something you want to talk about then?"

Now numerous blips appeared on the device and it spoke the word *Wheel*.

"Oh my, were you hurt by this large wheel?"

The device spoke again. *Killed.*

"You were killed by this wheel?"

More blips appeared on the device. It was as if whatever was there was trying hard to get their story across. Ellen felt the air around her get heavy. The next question just popped out of her mouth.

"Are you the woman that was murdered on these stairs by her husband?"

The Ghost Meter they had setup by the flywheel began to flash and beep like mad. Four red blips appeared on the Ghost Radar, and the word *Murder* seemed to almost scream from it, as if somehow the volume on the device had increased all on its own. At the same moment there was a scream from down the hallway. In one frantic motion Ellen jumped up and bolted down the stairs leaving all of the equipment behind at the sound of her daughters' voice. She called out back to her.

"Sarah!"

Sharon was frozen in place, she was almost unable to speak at this point. Sarah had stood up on her own deciding not to wait for Sharon's help. She took a couple steps away from the well and the shadow figure, hoping that would help reduce the sick feeling she had. It did not. She had heard Sharon tell her to take her hand, but when she turned to tell her she was already up, a wave disbelief and fear came over her. There between her and her friend was the tall dark shadow figure. It blocked out most of her view of Sharon but she could see Sharon's face and could see her friend was in shock. She heard Sharon quietly speak her name.

"S…S…Sarah."

Sarah could feel the anger and anxiety coming from the figure, although she did not know why or what the feelings were about, but seeing her friend in the state she was in, and knowing this thing was causing it made Sarah loose it. Her own fear immediately turned into anger and feelings of protection for her friend. Sarah looked inward and envisioned a bright white light expanding outward around her toward the shadow figure and Sharon. She screamed at the figure before her.

"Leave my friend alone! Get out of here! NOW!"

She envisioned the white light pushing it away and down into the well. The shadow figure vanished from in front of her. She could once again make out Sharon in the dim light of their flash lights. It was then she heard her mother yelling for her. She yelled back.

"We're here! Get down here, but be careful!"

Sarah did not want to say that they were okay, because she was not sure they were. She walked over to Sharon and put a hand on her shoulder, and spoke softly to her.

"Sharon? Are you okay?"

Sharon just stood, still a bit shocked by what had just happened. She looked down at her hand that something had taken a hold of. It was still ice cold and felt numb, like that pins and needles feeling when your arm or hand has fallen asleep.

"Yeah. Yeah I'm okay Sarah. I'm just a bit dumbfounded is all. I mean someone grabbed my hand. I know it wasn't you, but someone did. I mean I felt it. It gripped my hand, and it was ice cold!"

A shiver ran through her body, and she shook. She rubbed her hands together to try and warm the one up, and get the circulation back into it.

Ellen moved as quickly as she could through the maze of trash and debris in the hallway without killing herself, or falling and breaking a leg. She found Sarah and Sharon standing there talking, Sharon was rubbing her right hand and arm.

"Are you guys okay?! Sarah, I heard you screaming."

Sarah turned to look at her mother. Sharon looked up from rubbing her arm and hand, which were finally starting to warm up, and the circulation was beginning to come back.

"We just had a crazy experience down here with a dark shadow figure! It even grabbed me by the hand!"

The women went on to describe what happened to them in as much detail as they could remember. Ellen told the two of them what had been happening to her at the same time as their experience. Sharon spoke what they all were beginning to surmise.

"Given the two experiences, I would have to say we hit on something sinister here, and they're connected."

Sharon pointed to Ellen.

"I think you connected with the spirit of the murdered woman Ellen, and that stirred up the spirit of maybe the man that killed her, and that's who Sarah and I just dealt with."

Ellen looked at her, then nodded.

"Yeah, I agree, but we won't know for sure until we review everything we've collected on audio and video. It does seem that way though."

Sarah provided her own theory to the group.

"It could also be that we all interacted with the same spirit. I mean yes it made me sick, but it also took Sharon's hand when she offered it to me to help me up. It was a frightening experience, but what if it was just trying to reach out to all of us for help. I mean it didn't harm any of us. You know I'm sensitive to spirit, I may have just picked up on its pain and that's why I felt sick. We just don't know for sure yet."

Sharon was picking up some of their equipment they had left on the floor, including their flashlights. She handed Sarah's to her.

"Yeah, I hadn't thought of that. It is a possibility, and it did leave as soon as you yelled at it to go away. That doesn't seem like something an aggressive spirit would do."

Ellen picked up the hand-held camera that was sitting on the floor.

"Well, we will just have to see what the evidence shows us. Okay, so what do you guys want to do now? Have we had enough for one night, or do we want to do more?"

Sarah took the camera from her mother.

"Why don't we go back to basecamp, take a break and regroup and then decide what to do next. We can also find out what time it is since everyone's phones but Ellen's is back at basecamp."

Sharon agreed.

"Good point. Let's head back. Ellen we'll pick up your stuff on our way. Let's leave the rest of the equipment down here running for now and we can come back and get it later. We might still catch something else down here, which could give us more answers."

The three women turned and walked back towards the basement stairwell.

After returning to basecamp they found it was only 11:05 pm, so they made the decision to continue investigating, at least until 1:00 am. They spent rest of the night investigating the third floor offices. It was a large area and although some of the office walls had large holes in them from the ongoing construction, the walls allowed them to investigate individual areas of the floor without contaminating each other's EVP sessions. For the most part they stayed together anyway, but they did try one session where they were each in a separate room on the floor to see if being isolated would stir up any activity. They did at times get knock responses to questions, and both Sharon and Sarah heard a disembodied male voice, although they could not quite make out what it said. They also heard walking in the main hallway of the floor, but they were all sitting together in one room at the time, and the security guard was still back at his office. They checked everything out, but no one was there. They finished up their investigation at around 1:30 am, packed up all their equipment, contacted the guard to let them out, and then headed home.

Ellen spoke with Dan the next day to let him know how things had gone, and that they would review all of the evidence and get back to him within four weeks with their findings. It was during this conversation that Dan gave Ellen some very exciting news about a friend of his that was looking for a reputable paranormal team to come and investigate his property for him.

"So Ellen, this friend of mine lives in Connecticut. He owns a large parcel of property that has an old abandoned town on it, that's what he wants to have investigated. He gets trespassers on his property all the time because of all the stories and legends about the place. Maybe you've heard of it. It's the old ghost town of Barra-Hack, near Pomfret, Connecticut."

Ellen just about dropped her cell phone as she gave a quick yell of excitement.

"Oh my God! Are you kidding! Yes, I know that place! Yes, tell your friend we'll be honored to investigate it for him! I just need to call Jack and let him know! I want him there for that one, so we will have to wait until he is over this flu bug he has, but yes have your friend give me a call and we will work out all of the details!"

The Merrimac Paper Mill was an actual factory located on the banks of the South Canal of the Merrimack River in Lawrence, Massachusetts. As stated in the story it was originally built in 1886, and remained a working paper mill until 2005. It was bought and sold several times over the years, with attempts to re-purpose the property but without any success. On the evening of 13 January 2014 a massive fire broke out in the building, which was responded to by eight fire companies and over seventy fire-fighters from as far away as Lowell and Wilmington, Massachusetts. By the time the fire was contained around 6:30 pm the building was left gutted and nothing more than the outer walls were still standing. The long standing landmark of the Lawrence was gone. All that remains now are photos, historical documents, the memories of those that worked there, and the ghosts of her past.

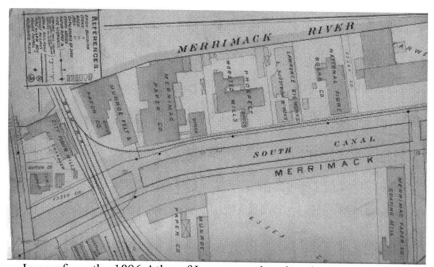

Image from the 1896 Atlas of Lawrence showing the location of the Merrimac Paper Company

The following photos were taken by the S.P.I.R.I.T.S. of New England team during their investigation on 28 April 2012. S.P.I.R.I.T.S. was the only paranormal team ever allowed to investigate the location. I personally do believe that during that investigation a spirit of the old mill did connect with one of our investigators, Sharon Koogler. She told me that when she saw the fire on the news she found herself crying, although she did not know why and it was completely unexpected. This is a typically a sign of a spirit connection. Picking up on the feelings and emotions of a spirit that is possibly attached, or at least has a strong connection with you.

From left to right: Sharon Koogler, Ellen MacNeil, and Sarah Campbell

The Catwalk inside the Merrimac Paper Mill

Looking down from the Catwalk

The Flywheel in the basement floor where the woman was
supposedly murdered

The basement hallway where shadow figures were seen by employees

The Well in the basement area

What Sharon Koogler dubbed "The Blair Witch Wall" in the basement of the Merrimac Paper Mill

To learn more about the history of the Merrimac Paper Mill and the fire you can do a Google search using the term "Merrimac Paper Mill Lawrence ma", or you can go to one of the following websites:

1. http://www.lawrencehistory.org/node/329

2. http://www.eagletribune.com/news/local_news/fire-destroys-historic-merrimac-paper-mill/article_25950e6b-0a33-5da3-b6e6-cda1765ef9dc.html - NOTE: This article includes photos of the fire.

3. https://youtu.be/ce_CFrEAo8o - Merrimac Paper Mill Fire Lawrence, MA 1/13/14

4. https://youtu.be/5V2l8Gnz9oc - Published on Sep 21, 2014 Quadcopter views of two ruined industrial buildings in Lawrence, Massachusetts: Merrimac Paper Company (built in 1860s, burned in 2009, 2010, and 2014).

5
THE BARA-HACK
INCIDENT

And at even, when the sun did set, they brought unto him all that
were diseased, and them that were possessed with devils.
Mark 1:32 - King James Version (KJV)

y lle hwn yn cael ei melltithio gan gythreuliaid - Welsh

It was a full moon but the storm clouds prevented even the slightest gleam of moonlight from shining through and lighting the partially overgrown trail into the old growth forest. Jack kept wondering to himself what the hell they were doing here.

His four friends and team mates; Ellen, Sarah, Sharon and Beck; had all convinced him this would be a once in a life time opportunity for their S.P.I.R.I.T.S. of New England paranormal team to investigate the infamous ghost town of Bara-Hack. This very old, and supposedly haunted ghost town was located in the sparsely populated northeastern region of Connecticut. Jack had read up on the history and folklore of town. He found out it is purported to be haunted by the spirits of the original founders of the town, Obadiah Higginbotham and John Randall, and that it was believed that over the years some satanic cults held rituals in ruins of the town, which had opened the door to demonic activity. A recent increase in trespassers had finally prompted the property owner to contact the S.P.I.R.I.T.S. team to team come out and investigate the location in hopes of settling once and for all if the old town was haunted or not.

The land owner himself had witnessed several unusual things at the old town that he just could not explain, including seeing shadow figures dart about between the trees, hearing the sounds of a horse drawn carriage coming down the old trail leading into the abandoned village, and hearing voices in the remnants of the town when he was clearly there alone.

It was a two-mile hike back into Bara-Hack from the start of the dirt access road behind the property owner's house. The dirt logging road quickly turned into an overgrown trail within the first 200 yards of their walk. Since the team could not drive back to the location they had to carry their equipment with them, that being the situation, they kept their investigation equipment to a minimum. They had packed two medium size backpacks filled with two mini-dv infrared camcorders, several digital audio recorders, a couple of KII meters and Mel-Meters for measuring electro-magnetic anomalies, flashlights, and lots of extra batteries. All of this would be used to capture a visual and audio record of their investigation, and attempt to record any evidence of spirit activity within the old ghost town. They also carried two other backpacks filled with food, drinks, a first aid kit, and of course…toilet paper. This was not going to be a typical investigation, the nearest home, road and help was two miles away from the site they were headed to.

Right now the flashlights, map, and a compass Jack had brought with him were the most important pieces of equipment they had, at least as far as Jack was concerned. Still the pitch black of the stormy overcast night and the overgrown trail did not make for easy going, and only turned what should have been a two-hour hike to the old town into a three-hour hike. A long time hunter and hiker, Jack's experience made him the obvious choice to lead the way. He stopped often to check the map and make sure everyone else was okay and still with him.

"Are you all still back there?"
Jack shined his flashlight back towards his friends. Ellen was the first to answer, sounding a bit winded.

"Yeah, we're here, but can we take a few minute break please?"
Jack shot back with a bit of sarcasm in his voice and a smirk on his face.

"Why, are you tired?"
Ellen snapped back at him.

"Wise ass!"
He could tell she was a bit annoyed with him. He snickered back at her.

"Hey, this was your idea not mine."
Sharon interrupted their friendly banter.

"Hey Jack, what time is it? How far are we from the ghost town?"
Jack took out his cell phone to check the time. While doing that he also noticed he did not have any cell signal.

"It's about 9:57 pm, and we should be just about there. I would say we only have about one-hundred yards or so to go. Hey does anyone have a cell signal on their phone?"
Everyone looked at their phones. No one had any signal. Jack put his phone away.

"Well that's just great. God help us if we need any help out here."
He stood in the overgrown trail checking over the map, then took his flashlight and checked out his other two friends and team members

to be sure they were also doing okay.

"Beck, Sarah are you both ok?"

Beck looked over at Sarah who was now sitting on an old stump next to her. Sarah gave Beck a quick nod indicating she was good, then Beck responded.

"Yeah, we're okay, we're still with ya."

Jack smiled, it made him feel a little better to know everyone was at least doing okay, even if they were a bit tired.

"Excellent! If you all want to, take 10 minutes and get something to drink for yourselves. I'm going to check ahead to make sure we stay on the trail, and look for the next marker. Like I said, I think we're just about there, but I'd feel better if I took a quick look ahead."

The ladies mumbled their agreement and Ellen jokingly added...

"Be careful and make sure you come back 'cuz we don't want to die out here by ourselves!"

Jack just gave a quick laugh and quipped back.

"Yeah, don't worry. I'll be back for ya."

He turned and began heading down the trail when he heard Sharon call out to him.

"Hey Jack hold up! I'm going with ya."

He was glad for the company and gave her a big smile.

"Great! It'll be good to have a second pair of eyes on the trail."

He was truly being grateful for the company. Something was starting to feel a little off to him. He felt like someone or something was watching them from the darkness of the woods. It sent an ice cold chill through his whole body.

Jack and Sharon had only walked about another sixty yards or so when Jack stopped abruptly, causing Sharon to walk right into him almost causing both of them to fall to the ground, which both startled and pissed Sharon off.

"Jesus Jack! Give me a warning next time will ya!?"

Jack snapped sharply back at her, but in a whispered tone.

"Shush! Quiet!"

Sharon could hear the urgency in his voice. She knew something was up. She spoke softly now trying to also hear whatever it was she thought Jack had heard.

"What is it? What do you hear?"

Jack was standing as if he was at attention. His eyes were shut as he was straining to block out anything that might distract him from listen again for what he thought he had heard.

"I thought I heard...it sounded like voices. Someone talking ahead of us."

Sharon immediately went into her debunking mode of trying to figure out a possible logical explanation for what he had heard. She was also hoping to come up with an explanation that was something other than the possibility that there were other people in the woods with them on a stormy night. The thought she was trying to avoid was that some crazy satanic cult was in the woods ahead of them. A chill went up her spine. She spoke quietly.

"Jack, are you sure it wasn't the rest of the team behind us?"

Jack knew what he had heard, mumbled voices along the trail just ahead of them.

"No, this was right in front of us. Not more than ten to twenty yards ahead."

Sharon got that chill again. She did not like the possible idea of strangers being in the woods with them.

"I don't know Jack. Sound can carry in these woods you know. It could have been..."

Jack cut her off. He turned and looked her straight in the eyes. He noticed that something looked different about Sharon's eyes, even about her face. He could not explain it, for she seemed more vivid, if that made any sense at all. He shook it off.

"It wasn't them, Sharon. These were male voices from in front of us. I know what I heard."

Sharon was slightly annoyed that Jack seemed to blow off her theory of it being Ellen, Beck and Sarah talking.

"Well I didn't hear them so I just don't know."

Jack could hear the tone in her voice and knew he had upset her. He could sense an odd intense vibe in the woods the closer they got to the old Bara-Hack settlement. He realized it was probably affecting him. He could tell Sharon was anxious as well. He calmed his voice as he responded to her.

"I'm sorry Sharon. I just know what I heard. You know me, I wouldn't insist on something if I wasn't sure about it."

Sharon backed her tone down as well. She knew he was truly sorry about snapping at her, and she knew he was also sensitive to picking up on energies and spirits at a location, and understood that might be what was affecting him as well.

"I know, but I'm just saying that I didn't hear the voices, so I have no way of knowing what you heard. If you did hear voices I'm also worried it could be peop…"

This time Sharon stopped herself in mid-sentence, she now heard the voices Jack was talking about.

"Holy crap! You're right Jack! Those are male voices and they're just ahead of us!"

Sharon shined her light toward the voices. There, less than thirty feet ahead of them stood two dark figures in the middle of the overgrown path.

"What the fu…"

Before Sharon could finish the two shadow figures darted off to the right and into the trees. Jack took off after them, he could tell just by their movement they were not people or animals, the two figures made no noise and seemed to just glide across the ground, they did not even disturb the tall weeds on the pathway or any branches as they moved swiftly through the trees, then they just disappeared.

Sharon stood there for a moment not sure what she had just seen. She ran after Jack and found him about thirty yards away standing near the fallen down stone walls of an old building, the wooden floor still visible inside the broken walls. Sharon touched Jack on the shoulder, he jumped!

"What the hell!"

Sharon laughed a bit.

"Ha! Sorry, sorry. Jack, are you ok?"

He turned to face her holding his hand on his chest, and trying to catch his breath after running through the dark woods.

"Yeah… Yeah I'm ok. I just wanted to see where those things were going."

Sharon looked around at the empty floor and then around at the dark woods. She could just barely make out some stone ruins within the small area around them. This was what was left of the old Bara-Hack settlement. Broken stone walls and foundations. Not really much to look at.

"Where did they go?"

Jack pointed to the old wooden floor in front of them. He took a deep breath to regain his composure and his breath before responding to her question.

"Right here. They disappeared right here inside this fallen down building. They seemed to just fade into the floor."

He looked back at her and saw the confusion in in her face.

"Was this the first time you ever saw shadow people Sharon?"

Sharon was taken aback by his question. She took a moment to process it.

"What?! Shadow people? Is that what those figures were?"

Jack had been hunched over a bit to help catch his breath. He now stood himself upright and a smile came across his face, with the realization that this was Sharon's first experience seeing not just one, but two shadow figures. He was kind of happy and excited for her, he also knew it would take her some time to process it.

"Yeah, they were shadow people. That's why they didn't make any noise when they took off and seemed to glide over the ground."

Sharon's face immediately changed expression, she now had a huge smile.

"Awesome! Woo Hoo! My first shadow people!"

Jack was a little taken aback by her response, it seemed out of place for her. He put his hand on her shoulder, and got a little serious with his tone.

"Yeah, well, it's not all fun and games with these things. They can be associated with bad stuff like angry spirits or even demonic type hauntings. I think we better get back to the girls and let them know what we just found. By the way, this is the town, we were closer than I thought. I find it a bit interesting and slightly unnerving that those things lead me right to it. Anyway, let's go grab the rest of the crew and start this investigation!"

In less than fifteen minutes Jack and Sharon had gathered the rest of the team and they were all standing outside the ruins of the building where Jack had watch the shadow figures disappear into the floor. Ellen stared at the floor for a bit and then asked an obvious questions based on what Jack had just told them.

"So they disappeared into the floor?"

Jack smiled, he knew she was tired from the long trek and was really just trying to get her thoughts together.

"Yeah, they just seemed to pass right through it at the far left back corner, over there."

Jack pointed to the location. Sharon made an obvious suggestion.

"Why don't we check it out and see if there's anything over there." She started to make her way across the dilapidated wooden floor towards the far corner he was pointing to. Jack was shocked, again this was not like Sharon. She would never do something as dangerous as walk across a rotten wooden floor. He yelled to her.

"Sharon! Hold on!"

He grabbed her arm as she stepped onto the rotted wood of the old floor and eased her back onto solid ground.

"I don't think we should just walk across this; it looks pretty unstable. Let's walk around the outside to that corner and we can check things out from there."

Beck gave Sharon the *you idiot* look, and then voiced her agreement with Jack.

"Good idea Jack."

They broke out some of their equipment, Jack took one of the mini-DV cameras. He knew they needed to start documenting all of this. They had already missed enough to this point. The team worked their way around the outside of the ruins to the far corner of what had once been a house. There were some stones and timber lying on the floor in that far corner but Sarah noticed something odd about the floor under them. There appeared to be a trap door in it, with a large metal ring attached to pull it open. Jack hesitantly stepped onto the floor, checked to see if it would hold his weight; it seemed to be much sturdier than it looked. He cleared away the debris to reveal the trap door Sarah had spotted. He stood on the side of it, took hold of the large iron ring and pulled up on it. The rusty latches creaked open as Jack lifted the heavy door. They all looked down into the void, it was pitch black inside. Just then there was a loud clap of thunder and flash of lightening that illuminated the woods and the darkness of the cellar below them. Jack jumped back and dropped the door at the sight of the face he glimpsed staring up at him from the darkness below.

"WHAT THE...!"

The others could see that Jack was shaken by whatever had just happened. Ellen went up to him and put her hand on his back.

"What is it?! Are you okay?! What did you see?!"

Ellen was concerned for him, she had never seen Jack react like that to anything on all the investigations they had done together. They all asked if he was ok.

"Yeah I...To be honest I'm not sure, I...I don't know."
Jack was a bit rattled. Sharon and Sarah spoke to him calmly.

"What did you see Jack? Can you describe it?"
Jack took a deep breath and composed himself, but still for a moment he could not speak, his mind was still trying to process what he believed he had seen.

"It was the face of an old man with a scraggly beard, his face drawn and dirty. He was smiling, but it was an awful smile, like one you would see on a killer just before he attacks his next victim."
Sharon was excited by what Jack described.

"Awesome! Looks like we're off to a great investigation! I know you had the mini-DV going when you opened the door, do you think you caught it on camera?"
Jack looked at her. He was baffled by her reaction to what he had seen. She was acting strangely ever since they had seen the shadow figures. Normally she would show much more concern and caution. He looked down at the camera he was holding.

"I don't know, maybe. Let's check and see."
He rewound the footage and played it back. What he saw on small screen of the camera was upsetting to say the least. The camera had captured something, but it was not the face that he had seen, this was even more unsettling. It was the image of a black mass with what appeared to be red eyes staring up at him from the darkness of the cellar. Beck saw it and freaked out.

"We need to get out of here now! Right now! We're not messing with this thing!"
Ellen attempted to calm her down.

"Beck relax. We won't stay here much longer, but we have to try and check some things out for our client."
Beck began walking away into the darkness of the woods, not even realizing what direction she was going.

"Not me! I'm out of here! I'm leaving right now!"
Jack yelled at her. He was very concerned at this point for everyone. No one was acting like themselves, Beck was usually the calm one and Ellen would be the one to refuse to stay and storm off. All he

could think is that it was these woods and whatever was inhabiting the ruins of this old town that was affecting everyone. A deep chill went through his whole body.

"Beck wait! You can't go alone you might get lost. Sarah go with her please."

He realized at this point there was no stopping Beck from leaving, but he could not let her wander off into the woods by herself, in the dark, with a storm looming. Sarah reluctantly agreed to go. Jack handed Sarah the map and his compass.

"Sarah, if all else fails, just follow the compass to the west and you'll walk out to route 169, from there you can walk back to the cars. But if you just take your time and stay on the trail and you'll be fine."

Sarah gave him nod, a thumbs up, and a look of confidence.

"You got it Jack. We'll be fine."

Then she turned and walked off with Beck down the trail. Once the girls were out of sight Sharon excitedly spoke up.

"Ok, now let's go investigate this creepy old cellar!"

Jack spun around to see Sharon and Ellen heading down into the cellar of the old ruin.

"No! Wait! Stop!"

Jack yelled to them, but he was too late, they disappeared into the darkness. The next thing he heard was Ellen saying that her flashlight was not working and Sharon saying something had pushed her. Jack ran to the open hatch in the floor. What happened next happened very quickly, so quickly that Jack's mind just went numb from it all. He seemed to just black out at one point. He remembered climbing down into the cellar after his friends to help them, it was total darkness and even his flashlight did not seem to penetrate the blackness. He remembered hearing Ellen scream, he remembered the black mass lunging at him, and he thought he remembered being knocked down onto the dirt floor by some unseen force. Then there were just flashes of something bright and metallic, mixed with flashes of red and black, and screams of pure terror and then...silence and darkness.

It was the strange creaking noises that woke him up, that and the blood rushing to his head. Jack found himself hanging upside down, his feet bound and the rope hanging from a large meat hook in one of the rafter beams of the cellar. His hands were bound behind his back and tied with another rope back to his feet. He could not move. He looked around the room as his eyes finally adjusted to the darkness. It was easier to see now; he could tell the sun had come up as small rays of light shown down through the cracks in the floor above. What he saw next horrified him. There were thick pools of blood everywhere, and there seemed to be some kind of odd mass piled in the corner in front of him. After gazing upon it for a bit he could make out body parts, human body parts, and a head with dark hair, but there was more than one body in that pile. He could now smell the blood and other bodily fluids emanating from the pile and the rest of the cellar. He was trying hard to hold back his compulsion to vomit. It was the low moan coming from the far corner of dank cellar that kept him from puking by giving him something else to concentrate on. His focus became more pronounced as he recognized the sound of the voice.

"Sharon is that you!? Sharon, answer me!"

He was trying to speak in a loud whisper, not knowing who or what else might be nearby. He could see the dark hunched figure in the corner slowly stand up, using one arm to lean on the dirty stone wall to brace itself as it stood up, then it turned around to face him. Jack could tell by the figures outline it was Sharon. Jack's heart began to race. Thank God she was still alive! Now they had a chance to get out of this living nightmare!

"Sharon, are you ok!? Come help get me down from here, and we'll get out of here!"

Then Jack heard the heavy footsteps on the wooden floor above them. His heart began to race as he began to panic! It had to be the thing they had encountered last night coming back to finish its gruesome job!

"Sharon hurry! Cut me down! We can still get out of this!"

It was then that the figure standing in the far corner lifted its head and opened its eyes. He saw their deep red glow from across the darkness. It was at that moment Jack realized that the dark figure was not his friend Sharon, at least not anymore. He could see the glint of the meat cleaver in its hand and could hear the dripping of the blood that coated it. He could also hear the sound of voices above them, he yelled out hoping he would be heard. The figure now raised the cleaver and lunged towards him, at the same moment the trap door to the cellar swung open and bright sunlight filled the room. Just for a moment Jack could see the face of his friend Sharon, twisted and distorted by the demon that now possessed her; he saw the cleaver come down at him to split him open. Then he heard a man yell, followed by a loud blast, his ears rang from the deafening sound in the confined space, then a more muffled second blast. He knew it was muffled only because his ears were still ringing from the first blast. He saw the body of what had once been his friend Sharon fall back and drop to the floor, in a dead lump. He felt a warm rush of liquid flowing down his chest and over his face. He strained to look up and saw the cleaver buried in his chest, the warm liquid was his own blood draining from him, taking his life with it. The last things he remembered were hearing more heavy footsteps clambering down the cellar stairs, feeling himself lifted up, carried up the cellar steps into the bright light of day, and then set down gently on the cool damp ground of the forest floor. He recognized the hat and badge of a State Trooper leaning over him and speaking to him, but he could not make out the words. He was surprised that he felt no pain. He was angry that he was not able to help his friends, and regretted that he had perhaps not acted fast enough that night to stop it all from happening. He hoped that Sarah and Beck had at least gotten away, but he knew that the pile of body parts he had seen meant more than one person had been murdered. He could feel that his arms were free now, the Officer had cut the bonds. He could feel the warm sun on his face. Then he saw a face he recognized. It was Sarah! She was alive! She was kneeling beside him talking to him, he tried to hear her words, but they were faint to him, like a whisper. She was crying. Sarah was kneeling beside him holding his hand. He focused on her face which suddenly became very vivid, just like Sharon's had the night before in the forest. She spoke two words to him that were surprisingly loud and very clear.

"Don't go!"

He looked at her and smiled, at least he felt like he was smiling. He used the last of his strength to reach up with his right hand and touch her face, wiping the tears from her cheek. She smiled back at him. Then the world began to glow brighter around him, he felt at peace, he no longer felt anything except the warmth of the light. Jack then felt like he was falling, then his whole body convulsed as if he had stuck his finger into a light socket!

The convulsion woke him from his sleep and he found himself home in bed. He was sweating profusely and his whole body ached. He could tell his fever had finally broken though. He reached for the thermometer on his nightstand and checked his temperature, 99.8°, much better than the 101.8° it had been when he went to bed. He sat up on the edge of the bed and rubbed the back of his neck.

"Damn nightmare."

He mumbled to himself as he sat there. He knew it was more than that though. It had been far too vivid. Far too real to be just a dream. It was a premonition. He had other vivid dreams like it before, but the giveaway that it was a premonition was the message at the end. In this case the one Sarah had given him. The reason he could hear her say "Don't go!" so clearly, and the reason her face was so vivid was because it was a message from his spirit guide, or perhaps even his guardian angel. He did not have the clarity yet to figure out what it meant, but he knew that would come in time, it always did. He jumped again when his cell phone on the night stand rang. He reached to answer it. He knew from the Exorcist ring tone it was Ellen.

"Hello."

He knew by the tone of her voice she was excited about something.

"Jack, its Ellen! Jesus you sound like shit."

Jack nodded his head slowly.

"Gee thanks Ellen. Good morning to you too. Yeah, I even look worse than I sound."

Ellen felt a little bad now. She had forgotten in her excitement that he was sick the last several days.

"I'm sorry. I hope you feel better soon. Anyway, guess what location we have just been asked to investigate!"

Jack already knew what it was, and just blurted it out.

"The Bara-Hack ghost town."

For a moment there was dead silence on the other end of the phone.

"How the hell did you know that!?"

Ellen sounded perplexed and upset.

"It's a long story Ellen and I'll tell you later I promise. This one we really need to discuss and think about before we say yes to it. You'll understand why when I talk with you later, but to be honest right now I'm not feeling very well."

He did not wait for Ellen to respond, he just hit the end call button and hung up on her. He would deal with it all later. He got up from bed, went into the bath room and vomited. Psychic events always took a physical toll on the body, and being sick did not help matters at all.

6
SEMJAZA

*So the devils besought him, saying, If thou cast us out, suffer us to go
away into the herd of swine.
Matthew 8:31 - King James Version (KJV)*

Another long day of work, followed by another long night of
work, at least he enjoyed the night job, well some of it anyway.
Reviewing evidence, while it could have its rewarding moments, for
the most part was as boring as watching grass grow, especially when
listening to audio from a case where he had set up multiple audio
recorders at a small location. You always end up listening to the same
conversations over and over again. It had its advantages though. On
more than one occasion he was able to debunk what he thought
might be an EVP on one recorder by having caught what was one of
his investigators whispering something to their partner on another,
but they had forgotten to tag it. This was not one of those cases
though. This case involved a huge home; one could say a mansion,
and a teenage boy who seemed to be experiencing spirit oppression
or possibly even an attachment or possession. Michael was a
seasoned paranormal investigator, and knew what to listen for when
it came to EVPs. The newest member of his team was not too bad at
it either. She seemed to have a knack for picking up on things that
just seemed out of place. Recently he began thinking that is what had
attracted her to him.

Michael had begun investigating the paranormal at the young age
of seventeen with his grandfather and his team S.P.I.R.I.T.S. of New
England. He had started out by helping his grandfather review
evidence and conducting research for the teams' cases. When he got
older his granddad allowed him to start helping out on the
investigations themselves, and he learned everything he could about
the tech stuff, and different styles and methods of investigating. In
retrospect, he had actually been a reluctant draftee into the field of
paranormal research. Unlike most investigators who had gotten into
the field because of their passion for investigating the unknown, or
because they had their own experiences, he had just grown up with it.
While staying with his grandparents for a week one summer while his
parents were away, Jack, his granddad, just came to him one evening,
tossed a pair of headphones at him and said "Come on, you're going
to help me review some evidence."

He learned a lot in the years that followed and he found he had a knack for it, all of it, from evidence review to working with the clients. In Michael's case he "found" his passion for the paranormal. Like his grandfather, his biggest passion was in helping the people and families who believed they were experiencing paranormal activity. Helping people to understand what they just could not comprehend or feared. He helped them turn their fear into understanding. He helped these people not only understand what they were experiencing but how to deal with it, and in some cases, live with it, or rid themselves of it. Some cases were not as easy as others though. Some cases were just downright dangerous, and even scared the hell out of him sometimes. Luckily they were few and far between, but you just never knew when you might run into one of those "darker" cases. Something that might perhaps be demonic in nature. It was these types of cases that led him into a portion of the field that even his grandfather tried to avoid, Demonology. Somehow over the last seventeen years Michael now found himself as one of the most renowned and respected Demonologists in the paranormal field, and the truth was he was not even sure how it had happened. All he really knew was that he was trying to help people with problems they could not understand and did not know where else to turn to for help. That was the most important thing that he had learned from his grandfather, helping people is what matters in this field the most.

Michael glanced over at his investigator in training. Sarah was a young woman of twenty-seven. She was a redhead, about five foot seven inches tall, one-hundred-twenty-five pounds, and green eyes. She was smart, level headed, fun to hang out with and seemed to have a talent for identifying EVPs. He also found her to be one hell of an attractive woman. As if she could feel Michael's eyes on her, Sarah glanced up at him from her computer across the table and smiled, then looked back down at her work. Damn, he thought, she has a great smile too. He knew what was beginning to happen, he was falling for her and he hated to admit it. He had always kept one hard, fast rule for himself, never, ever date anyone on the team or at work. There had been others he was attracted to for sure, but he had always followed his rule, but this time was different, Sarah was different. He let out a deep breath and looked back down to his own computer at the audio file streaming slowly by in front of him.

Sarah heard him sigh and glanced back up at him. He was now

looking down at his computer screen. She stared at him for bit and her mind began to wander. She loved investigating the paranormal. You could say she was passionate about it, and being able to do it on the team of one of the most famous and well respected Demonologists in the field was just plain awesome! Being able to learn from the best of the best was not just an honor, but a dream come true. It had not happened by chance though; Sarah did not believe in leaving things to chance. Thirteen months earlier she had attended a paranormal event that Michael was speaking at. Since the event was being held at the hotel where she was working as a receptionist, she was able to find out what room he was staying in. The next morning after the first nights event she went up to his room bringing breakfast from the hotel restaurant with her. She knocked on the door stating she was with room service. When he answered, looking a bit confused because he had not ordered room service, she told him that it was compliments of the hotel. Before he had a chance to respond she told him who she was, that she was fascinated with the paranormal, and had been following his work for years. She suddenly realized that she had just made herself sound like a stalker or even worse, a paranormal groupie. She was surprised when he smiled and told her that if she could break away from work for a bit he would be glad to meet her in the hotel lobby in about an hour and talk with her. What she did not know about Michael at that time is that he was always willing to talk with people who were interested in or passionate about the paranormal. He loved the opportunity to encourage a person to explore the unknown and broaden their horizons. Of course Sarah jumped at the offer. After a bit of an awkward goodbye, she waited until he shut the door and then ran down the hallway grinning from ear to ear and went directly to the lobby where she sat waiting for an hour until he showed up, although she never told him that.

She did not expect what happened next either. They talked for over two hours about her interest in the paranormal, what she knew about investigating, her own personal experiences with it, and her personal insights about life, death, and the afterlife. Then he invited her to meet him and some of his team for dinner. At dinner he introduced her to the rest of his team and they all sat talking, eating and laughing together for the next few hours. She was a bit surprised by all of the questions Michael's team members were asking her, while for the most part Michael just sat back listening, smiling and making a joke from time to time. Before the three-day event was over, one of Michael's team members asked for her email address so they could keep her up to date on various events they would be doing. Three days after that, Sarah received an email from Michael himself asking her to give him a call. She was a bit nervous about calling him, wondering what it could possibly be about, and then she began to put two and two together. She had told his team at dinner that she envied them being on such a great team and sincerely wished that she could be one of them. She suddenly got excited and began shaking as she picked up her phone to call him. When he answered she found herself tongue-tied. Michael saw the number on his caller ID and finally broke in on Sarah's "Uh, uh..."

"Hello Sarah. How are you? I'm very glad that you called me."
Still all Sarah could get out was...

"Uh, yeah."
Michael was amused by her response, and then realized that she might have figured out why he asked her to call him.

"Sarah, are you ok?"
Sarah stammered.

"O...Oh God yes. Yes, I'm fine. I'm sorry."
Michael smiled.

"It sounds like you already figured out why I wanted you to call me."
Sarah could almost see the smile on his face over the phone. She could feel the tension winding up inside her like a taunt rubber band.

"Yes, I think I do! At least I'm praying that I do!"
Michael could hear the nervousness in her voice. He loved it and he wanted to drag it out for just a little bit longer. He knew she was a high energy individual, and he knew how big a deal this would be to her, and looked forward to hearing her reaction over the phone.

"So........."
Michael hesitated for just a moment longer, and if you asked him even to this day, he would swear he could feel the excitement building up in Sarah over the phone. He continued.

"Would you like to become a member of our team?"
There was dead silence on the other end of the phone, followed by a slowly building and jubilant scream.

"YYEEESSSSSSS!!!!!! OH MY GOD!!!!! YES!!!! WOOHOO!!!"

Sarah suddenly realized how loud she had screamed into the phone, right in Michael's ear! She was crying and laughing at the same time.

"OH MY GOD! I'm so sorry Mr. Kenna!"

Sarah began apologizing for blasting out his ear, but she began to calm down once she could hear him laughing on the other end.

"That's ok Sarah, and you can call me Michael, ok."

Again she could hear his smile through the phone.

"Ok, Michael. Again I'm sorry for screaming in your ear."

"That's ok Sarah, I totally understand."

Within a week Sarah found herself in the office of Rensselaer Paranormal Research, or RePR for short, being given a crash course on the team's inner workings. Thirteen months later she was still an investigator in training but she knew it was only a matter of weeks before she became a full-fledged investigator. She had achieved what she had set out to do, to become a member of one of the best paranormal teams in the world, but what she also found was something she had never even thought of, she found herself falling for Michael, which was not too hard to do for her given his well-built six-foot frame, thick dark hair, bright hazel eyes, compassion and love for others, and he was also the most confident man she had ever met, and was well respected by everyone who knew him. He also knew how to be respectful to others even when they maybe did not deserve it, and he was always encouraging people to follow their passions. Sarah could also tell that he was more than just a little interested in her as well. For now, they had a case to focus on and data to review. She snapped herself back to reality when she heard something obviously out of place in the audio file she was reviewing. She looped that section of the audio and listened to it twice more. Then she tapped on top of Michael's laptop to get his attention.

Michael was intent on listening to his own audio, when he felt his laptop move. Then he heard Sarah saying his name.

"Michael. Michael."

Sarah spoke softly while tapping on the laptop. Michael paused his audio and took off his headphones.

"What's up Sarah?"

Michael still had an intent look on his face and he could see Sarah had the same look on hers.

"Michael, I think I've got something here. As a matter of fact, I know I do. It's very odd though, like a language I've never heard before, but the voice is clear and to be honest it sounds a bit angry."

Michael reached out his hand and Sarah handed him her head phones.

"Play it for me please."

He closed his eyes and listened intently. He did not need to. What he heard next sent a cold chill up his spine.

"Play it again Sarah."

He really did not need to hear it twice, he knew what he had heard, but his mind just did not want to accept it, not just yet anyway. After the second time he pulled the head phones off and dropped them onto the table in front of Sarah. He rubbed the heels of his hands into his eyes.

"Michael what's wrong? What did you hear?"

She was concerned by his reaction.

"Fuck!"

Was all Michael said.

"What is it? What's going on?"

The concern in Sarah's voice brought him back. He looked up at her.

"Well you definitely found something. Something I hoped I would never hear again to be honest."

Michael recognized the look of confusion on Sarah's face. He explained.

"Do you remember the case that I dealt with seven years ago?"

She nodded in recognition.

"What you found Sarah is not good, not good at all. It's a voice all right, one that I'm very familiar with, and before you ask. Yes."

He took a deep breath before continuing.

"It's demonic, and it knows me."

He looked her in the eyes; he could see the fear, worry, and anxiety in them.

"Sarah, it's going to be ok, don't worry."

That was not true and he knew it, and he knew that she knew it too, but it at least sounded reassuring. Sarah was quiet; she did not know what to say at first. She was not sure it really made sense, but she felt terrible for finding the EVP.

"Michael I'm sorry."

Now it was Michael that was confused. There was a bit of a laugh in his voice, a nervous laugh.

"Sorry for what Sarah? It's not your fault."

She still felt awful about finding it. She knew that was ridiculous though, after all this is what they were here for, to review the data and see if they could find anything that would help them identify if the reported activity was paranormal or not, in order to help the people that looked to them for answers. She crossed her arms and leaned back in her chair.

"Ok, so what do we do now?"

Michael's answer was matter of fact and to the point. He leaned forward and stared straight into her eyes.

"We finish reviewing the rest of the data, and then we go back and help this family."

Sarah sat back up in her chair. She knew what that look and serious tone of his meant. It meant it was time to hunker down and get the job done. She was still curious about the EVP though.

"So what did you hear? What does the EVP say?"

He knew her. She was not going to drop it until he told her.

"If you listen to it again you'll hear it. It's a message for me. I know this because it calls me by name."

Sarah shook her head in disagreement.

"I didn't hear your name. It sounds like a different language."

Michael just smiled.

"No, it's English. It's just speaking backwards."

What Sarah heard was…

"leahcim ruoy luos si enim!"

Michael's cell phone chimed, it startled both of them. Michael answered even though it was almost midnight.

"Hello. Yes Mrs. Casey it's Michael, is everything ok? I see. Yes. Stay out of the room and we'll be there as quick as we can. Goodbye."

He looked at Sarah and could see she was nervous. He stood up and grabbed his coat off the back of his chair and put it on. He spoke to her calmly but firmly as he grabbed his small black and silver equipment case as he headed for the door.

"Sarah, start calling the rest of the team and tell them to meet me at Mrs. Casey's house within an hour. Tell them we have a demonic on our hands, and to be prepared for a long night, and Sarah. I think you should stay behind on this one."

Sarah was already calling the first team member when she glared at him in response to his last statement. She yelled at him before he could walk out the door, he stopped and looked back at her. He knew he should have kept going, but this was Sarah, and he had a great deal of respect for her.

"Michael! There's *no way* I'm not going with you, all of you, on this case! I'm part of this team and I'm sure as hell not letting you out of my sight on this one! Not after hearing that message from this *thing* on that audio! I'll be damned if I'm going to let anyone take your soul from ME!"

Michael smiled. He saw the intense look on her face, heard the commitment in her voice, her whole body was shaking, he noticed the quiver in her lips, and so there it was, out in the open for him to see. She had not said the words, but it was obvious none the less, she loved him and was going to stand by him no matter what. He also knew that strong words and strong emotions can be fleeting things, especially when confronted by pure evil. He had seen more than one supposedly *committed* team member break and run once confronted with a real demonic haunting. He knew now that Sarah loved him, but would that be enough for her to hold her ground once the shit hit the fan with this demon? They would both have to wait to find that out. His shoulders relaxed, he smiled and spoke gently and clearly back to her.

"Okay Sarah. Okay. Finish making the calls to the team and then grab that other equipment case in the corner and meet me out in my car. I'll wait for you, I promise. I won't leave without you."

An hour later Michael, Sarah, and the rest of the team; Robert, Jeff, Olivia, Beth, and Abby; were assembled in the Casey home living room. Mrs. Casey was in tears on the couch and two of his team members were trying to console her. Growling, banging and other ungodly sounds could be heard coming from upstairs in the home.

"Mrs. Casey."

Michael spoke softly to her. He truly felt heartbroken for the poor woman.

"Please believe me when I tell you we are going to do everything in our power to help your son and your family."

Mrs. Alice Casey was a woman in her early forties, an attractive woman by anyone's standards, about five-foot-seven-inch, one-hundred-ten-pounds, long sandy blond hair, and bright blue eyes. She had two children, both teenagers. A son, Jeremy, age fifteen and a daughter, Megan, age seventeen. Her husband David was also a good looking gentleman. Dark hair, hazel eyes, well built from working out regularly and a man of wealth. He was the owner of a well know import/export business dealing in fine antiques and art works, which was why he was not home. He was away in Japan and had been for the past three weeks. Their daughter was with him. After initially meeting Michael and his team, David became upset, he felt all this paranormal stuff was just B.S. and did not want anything to do with it. He felt their son was just sick and acting up to get attention. He was tired of his son's "antics" and of him terrorizing his sister. He told his wife to do what she felt had to done, but that neither he nor Megan would be staying around to watch the "freak show". Michael had seen this before on other cases, to him it was nothing new nor did it bother him. He knew this was typical of demonic activity. Drive the family apart in order to isolate the afflicted individual to gain total control and complete its' ultimate evil agenda. To destroy the family and force the possessed individual to lose all hope and take their own life. Given Mr. Casey's business, Michael felt it was very possible that it was one of the many antiques in the home that may be responsible for their son's current affliction. Spirit and even demonic attachment is always a real possibility when it comes to antiques.

Michael placed his right hand on Mrs. Casey's shoulder. She looked up at him, her eyes bloodshot and raw from crying. Michael looked empathetically into her eyes.

"Mrs. Casey, Alice, we will not turn our backs on you. Alice, I need to know what happened since we were here two weeks ago."

Mrs. Casey put her hand on his. Michael took her hand and sat on the couch next to her. He never took his eyes from her.

"Just take a breath and tell us whatever you can about what's been happening."

Michael glanced up at Jeff who was standing behind Mrs. Casey.

"Jeff, do you have a recorder on you?"

Jeff nodded.

"Yeah, it's been on since we got here. It's right there on the coffee table."

Michael smiled at him. He should have known better than to even ask the question. His team were professionals and they acted as such.

"Perfect. Thank you."

He turned his attention back to Mrs. Casey.

"Alice do you mind if we record this?"

She took a deep breath and nodded her consent.

"Yes. Yes, it's alright."

He smiled at her and squeezed her hand softly.

"Thank you. Just start with what you can remember."

She took another deep breath to gain her composure and began to tell all that had happened since they were last there doing their investigation.

"Well, after you all left things were quiet for a few days. Jeremy even seemed much better, less angry. He almost seemed happy. He even had a nice conversation with his father and sister on the phone. I thought maybe the house cleansing you did had gotten rid of whatever was here and afflicting him. Then last Friday he asked me if he could have his friend from school over. Things seemed so much better, I didn't see any harm in it. Really I didn't. I mean if I had known...."

She began to break down again. Michael gently squeezed her hand again with both of his.

"It's okay. It's going to...."

Mrs. Casey cut him off. Crying she forced herself to continue with the details of what had happened.

"That's just it Michael. It's not okay. It's not going to be. His friend from school was a sweet young girl Michael. She is only sixteen. She is one of his classmates. I didn't think anything of it when he told me they were going upstairs to his room to talk and play video games. If I had any idea, any at all of what he had planned, of what he was going to do to her... I... I...."

She broken down again. Everyone in the room was dead silent. They were all dumbfounded by this revelation. Michael was about to speak when Alice looked up at him. She looked directly into Michael's eyes and her tone became firm and straight forward.

"Anyway. A few hours later he came back down stairs, alone, a huge smile on his face, his eyes were... Well he... He... He didn't seem... He told me to go up to his room and see what "my son" had done to that little... bitch. I didn't know what to do... I went to his room... I called for an ambulance... the police came... He was in the mental ward until three days ago... They refused to keep him there... said he was a danger to the other patients and staff. The court had one of those tracking bracelets put on him. Said he's under house arrest because he's seventeen... my God he's only seventeen... how could he do such things to that poor innocent girl... That's not my son Michael... that THING up there is NOT my son!"

Everyone in the room was horrified by what Mrs. Casey had just told them. Michael could see she was forcing herself to go on. She was on the brink of insanity herself, he could see it in her eyes. He knew she was right about one thing. Whatever was up in that room was NOT her son, but he had a damn good idea what, and maybe even who, it really was. He reached up and placed his hand gently on Alice's face. She broke down and wept uncontrollably into Michaels arms. He hugged her tight. He looked up from Alice and to his team, specifically to Robert and Jeff. It always amused him how they looked like bouncers or mob thugs. They were both always well dressed with white shirts, dark suit pants, and black dress shoes. They were cousins and loved to work out and play sports, so they were both well built. Both were over six-foot tall, although Jeff was the shorter of the two. Jeff had his Master's degree in engineering, and Robert worked for the postal service. Both were good men and his best friends.

"Robert, Jeff, come with me. It's time to go to work."
Robert nodded and Jeff responded.

"Sure thing boss."
Michael looked to Olivia to take his place with Mrs. Casey. Olivia, or Livy as her friends called her, had been with the team for three years now. She was twenty-six, a Physician Assistant with long auburn hair, olive skin, green eyes, and a five-foot-eight-inch athletic frame, all of which made her a force to be reckoned with when she needed to be. She switched places with Michael to comfort Mrs. Casey. As he stood up Sarah grabbed him by the arm and stared deep into his eyes.

"I'm going with you."
He heard the determination in her voice. He was not about to argue with her.

"Ok Hun, but understand what you're in for? Once we enter that bedroom and close that door behind us we are committed. You have to do *exactly* what I say. Do you understand me?"
Sarah had never seen this look on Michael's face before. It was stone

cold serious, intimidating. The look alone said what he did not verbalize, that this is nothing like anything you have ever experienced before. This is dangerous, even deadly. If you're not ready for this, then walk away now before it's too late.

"Yes, I understand, and I'm ready."
She continued staring into his eyes.

"Ok then."
Michael looked away from Sarah to the rest of his team. He nodded to Robert and Jeff and they each grabbed a small case and headed back into the main hall of the huge home and up the marble staircase towards the bedroom where the growls, scratching and banging were emanating from. Michael then turned to another of his team; Beth, a twenty-five-year-old, black haired, five-foot-five-inch tall, stocky built young woman and Wiccan from northern Massachusetts, whom also had the unique ability to sense things that were out of the ordinary. She was no psychic, at least not yet, and nor did she claim to be, but she was open to the spirit world.

"Beth, I know you want to be in there with us, but I need you out here. I need you to go through the entire house and try to find the item that this thing came into the home through. You know what I'm talking about. Find me that item. It's critical that you do."
Beth knew exactly what he was talking about, find the item that contained the spirit portal or the demonic attachment.

"You got it Michael."
She knew exactly what she would need to find it.

"Abby."
He looked to the last member of his team, also a newer member like Sarah. Abby was thirty-one years old, single woman with long red hair, five-foot-seven-inches tall, and average build. She wore glasses which made her look like a teacher or librarian, she was actually a divorce lawyer by trade, which kind of made Michael scratch his head. He had never in all his years seen a lawyer have any interest in being a paranormal investigator. She was unique for sure, and extremely intelligent, and he was glad to have her on the team.

"I need you to assist Beth. She'll show you what to do, just follow her lead, ok?"
He could see the fear in her face and hear it in her voice as she responded.

"Ok Michael."

He could even see that she was trembling a bit. Abby was clearly scared, but he knew her fear had nothing to do with what was going on in the upstairs bedroom. He knew she was afraid of letting him and the rest of team down when they needed her the most. Michael paused for a moment, smiled and took Abby's hand.

"Abby, you're a good investigator and good researcher. You know what you're doing. It'll be fine."

She nodded and gave a whispered "Ok." and smiled back at him. Michael turned back to Sarah.

"You ready kid?"

Her response was short and quick, but he could hear the resolve in her voice.

"Yep."

They turned and headed upstairs.

The group stopped for a moment outside the boys' bedroom. Michael handed each of his team a silver necklace with a small medallion that had odd writing in a circular pattern on it.

"Wear these at all times while we're in that room."

Michael nodded towards the boys' bedroom.

"It will help protect you."

Then he said a short prayer with them before entering the room.

The bedroom was pitch black and the smell of sulfur and raw sewage permeated the air. Sarah started to gag but caught herself and held it back. She heard the door close and latch behind them as Michael locked it. The reality of it all sent a chill up Sarah's spine as she realized there was no going back now, but she did not plan to anyway. She was not going to leave Michael's side. Not now, not ever.

"Sarah."

Michael spoke quietly to her.

"Stay close to Jeff and Robert and follow their lead."

Sarah shot softly back to him.

"I'm staying by you Michael."

He turned and glared at her. He yelled at her in a whispered tone.

"Sarah! Do as I say!"

She was momentarily surprised by his reaction, then she remembered she had just promised to do as he said, and she had broken that promise within the first few moments of entering the room.

"Ok Michael, I'm sorry."

She was ashamed and angry with herself. Michael could see it in her face.

"Sarah, please just do what I ask. It's important if we are to be successful here, and safe."

Michael's voice lowered again and she could see his eyes pleading with her to do as he asked. There was a sudden loud thumping coming from within the room. The boy was nowhere to be seen. Then without warning the entire twin size bed; mattress, frame and all; flipped up from the floor and hurled towards the four of them.

Jeff and Robert had been at the front of the group. They both yelled "Look out!" and dove out of the way at the same moment. Michael shoved Sarah to the right and she fell to the floor. The bed hit Michael head on and knocked him into the door and onto the floor, with the bed laying half on top of him. The bed had hit him with such force that when it knocked him back into the solid oak door of the bedroom, the door split down the center. A very loud, high pitched laugh filled the room. Sarah, Jeff and Robert scrambled on their hands and knees over to Michael. Robert and Jeff lifted the bed off of him as Sarah positioned herself behind him and placed his head in her lap.

"Michael! Michael! Oh my God! Michael!"

Sarah was frantic. Michael opened his eyes.

"Michael, buddy, you ok?"

Jeff knelt down beside his friend, looking him over for any bleeding or possible broken bones.

"Yeah…Yeah, I think so…I'm ok. Are all of you ok?"

Michael attempted to get up but found himself being held down by Sarah. He looked up at her. Even in the dark room he could tell she was crying.

"Sarah, it's ok. I'm ok. I need you to let me up."

She leaned down and kissed him on the forehead and then on the lips. He kissed her back.

"Michael."

Robert reached down and grabbed him by his upper arm.

"Now's not the time for this man."

Michael looked up at him as both Robert and Jeff helped him to his feet.

"You're right Robert."

Michael looked to Sarah.

"Sarah, I do love you, but…"

There he had said it and put it out on the table for everyone to see. It was a dangerous move given the current company they were in. It could be used against them and he knew it, but it could also make them a stronger force for this thing to have to deal with.

"…we have to focus. This is a very dangerous and powerful force we're dealing with. We can't afford any distractions. Even this conversation is putting us all at risk. This thing is listening and it will use it against us if it can."

Just then Jeff, Sarah and Michael's walkies chirped to life and Beth's voice came crackling through.

"What the hell's going on up there?! Is everyone alright?!"

They could all tell that Beth was frantic.

"Beth, this is Jeff, everything is ok. We're all ok. *Do not* come up here. Keep searching for that object please."

"Ok, Jeff. Will do. I'll contact you as soon as we find it."

"Roger that Beth."

Sarah and Michael were both on their feet now with Jeff and Robert standing on each side of them. Michael stared deeply into Sarah's eyes. He wanted desperately to pull her to him and kiss her, but this was not the time or place for that. Robert turned to Jeff.

"Man, this isn't good. We all need to focus here before this thing kicks our asses again."

Michael turned away from Sarah and told her again to stay close to Robert and Jeff. She straightened herself out and went to stand by Robert. The four of them stood and turned toward where the bed had been. There was only the empty floor.

"Scan the room everyone, he's here somewhere."

Michael ordered while pulling his flashlight from his pocket. Jeff found the light switch on the wall, but it was not working, he had figured it would not be, but it was worth the try. The room seemed to be getting darker to all of them. Robert noticed that he could barely see Sarah who was standing only two feet from him but was moving away. He whispered to her.

"Sarah, stay close, don't wander in here."

It was huge for a bedroom, twenty-five-feet by twenty-feet. The furniture in the room barely helped to fill the space. With their flashlights they could see a recliner chair in the far left corner of the room, to the left of the chair against the wall was a computer table with a laptop. In the far right corner against the back wall was a large seven drawer dresser; on the right wall was a sliding glass door that lead out to a second floor balcony. The wall behind Robert and Sarah was filled with posters of rock bands, scantily clad female models, sci-fi movies and a few photos of a cute teenage girl, perhaps the one this thing had attacked. The wall on the opposite side of the entrance door was pretty much the same, with the exception of a large antique mirror smack dab in the middle of it.

"Where the hell is this kid!?"

Sarah, Jeff and Robert all jumped at the sudden sound of Michael's voice breaking the silence of the dark room.

"Damn Michael! You scared the crap out of me man!"

Robert was breathing heavy.

"Sorry everyone, but can anyone tell me why we can't find this kid!?"

Sarah had noticed something on the left wall that the others had missed.

"Michael check out that tall poster near the right corner of the left wall, just near the chair."

The three men all frantically swung their flashlights to it at the same time. They all breathed a sigh of relief when they saw nothing but a poster.

"It's just a poster Sarah."

Sarah was annoyed by their inability to see what she believed to be obvious.

"No Michael, it's not. There's a door behind it."

Michael moved closer to it, sure enough behind the huge poster was a door. The bottom of the poster did not touch the floor and so the base of the door was visible, you just had to look. Michael moved the poster aside and grabbed the door handle.

"Be careful man."

Robert whispered to him. All of them had their flashlights trained on Michael and the door. Michael had his pointed at the door so it would illuminate whatever was on the other side once he opened it. He knew that it was likely a closet, but probably a large one or even a walk-in closet based on the size of the bedroom. He pushed the door open slowly, just a crack at first, then more, and more, until it was opened enough for him to step inside. It was as he thought; a huge walk-in closet. He stepped inside.

No one moved as Michael disappeared, alone, into the closet. A moment later there was a loud bang followed by crashing noises coming from the closet.

"Michael!"

Sarah yelled as she and her team mates all ran towards the closet.

"It's ok, I'm ok. I just banged my head on a shelf and knocked a bunch of stuff over."

Michael was standing at the far end of the closet rubbing the top of his head. Sarah and Jeff stepped inside with him, training their flashlights on him. Michael took his hand from his head and held it palm out towards them.

"See mom, no blood. I'm good."

Jeff shined his light around the closet.

"So he's not in here either?"

Michael quipped back.

"No, he's not, but he has to still be in this room somewhere."

All at once the three of them turned their heads back towards the closet door. What had grabbed their attention was an odd, deep, low growling sound coming from within the bedroom, back where Robert was now standing in the dark all by himself. But this odd growl seemed mixed with another sound, something like gasping, as if someone was drowning or suffocating and trying desperately to catch their breath. Michael pushed both Sarah and Jeff aside and burst through the closet doorway. Michael searched frantically around the room with his light to find the source of the sounds. He could no longer hear the growling but could still hear someone gasping for their life's breath.

"Robert!"

Michael yelled into the darkness.

"Robert, answer me if you can!"

It was at that moment that Michael heard a faint and garbled "help" to his right. He turned and put his light on the source of the voice. There, four feet off the floor, pinned to the far wall like Christ crucified to the cross, was Robert. Michael lost it.

"LET HIM GO YOU BASTARD!!! IN THE NAME OF JESUS CHRIST, LET HIM GO!!!"

Michael did not know it, but Sarah and Jeff had been right behind him out of the closet and had spotted Robert even before he had. They were both frozen in place, just starring at Robert like a deer staring into the headlights of an oncoming car. They could not bring themselves to look away, they were in shock.

Robert's face was now turning blue from lack of oxygen. His eyes were rolling up into his head and he was passing out. Michael had grabbed onto Robert's waist belt trying to pry him down from the wall. He turned, glaring at Sarah and Jeff.

"Don't just fucking stand there! Help me for Christ sake!"
Michael's plea snapped Jeff out of his trance and he ran to help but Sarah was still frozen, dumb struck by what she was seeing, her brain not totally able to comprehend the reality of what was happening. She wanted to move, to run and help free Robert, but her body refused to take any commands she was giving it. It was at that moment that she knew exactly what the term "frozen with fear" truly meant.

Without any warning, while Michael and Jeff were struggling with all their might to free their friend from the wall, Robert's body went limp and fell onto the two men, crashing all three of them to the floor. Michael rolled out from under his friends' limp body and in one swift motion knelt beside him, gently slapping him on the face to try and wake him up, but there was no response.

"Robert. Robert. Come on Robert, wake up. Robert!"
Still no response. Robert's face was still bluish in color. Michael bent over his friend, positioned him flat on his back and tilted his head back a bit. He reached into his throat to check for any obstructions, he found one. He could feel the shape of it. He managed to get two fingers on it, and as gently as possible pulled it out of his friends' throat. It was the medallion and chain that he had given his friend to protect him.

There was no time for regret, he tossed it to the floor and began giving his friend mouth to mouth. A few moments later Robert began coughing and gasping as the life came back into him. A deep and growing growl came again from within the room. This time it was very easy to identify the direction the sounds was coming from. It was coming from the easy chair, directly behind Sarah. Michael motioned to Jeff.

"Jeff, I need you to get Robert on his feet and get him out of this room."

Jeff just stood there for a moment, still a bit out-of-sorts by all that had just occurred. Michael raised his voice to him.

"Jeff do you hear me!?"

Jeff looked at him and nodded his understanding. Michael spoke firmly and quietly.

"Do it now."

Robert had landed on Jeff hard and knocked the wind out of him. He was sitting up now, but was still a bit winded. He glanced up at Sarah, at first thinking that the growling had come right from her, but now realized it was from the chair behind her. Michael was now getting upset with Jeff's lack of action, he yelled at him.

"Jeff! Now! Get Robert out of here!"

Jeff turned his legs under him so he was on his knees next to Robert. He looked at Michael.

"But, what about...?"

Michael interrupted him, and continued to help him get Robert to his feet.

"Don't worry about us, just get Robert out. You need to get him to the hospital."

Jeff knew Michael was right, getting their friend to safety and medical help had to take priority.

"Ok, boss. Ok. But I'll be back, I promise."

Michael knew his friend was partly out of it, he thought that Jeff might even have a concussion himself, but he was still annoyed with him.

"Damn it Jeff just look after Robert!"

With that the two men got Robert onto his feet. Michael made sure Jeff had a good grip on Robert before letting go. The growling got louder as the two men moved towards the bedroom door. Michael dragged what was left of the bed away from the door and opened it for his two friends. The growling grew louder, angrier. Michael looked at his friends; Robert was finally coming around and semiconscious but still could not speak. Jeff was silent. Michael looked at them both. "Go" was all he said. Robert's eyes were glassy, but Michael could see he was nearly in tears, he looked over at Jeff. Jeff nodded his recognition of Michael's command, and gave a slight smile to his friend as he managed his way out the door with Robert hanging on to his shoulder. Michael slammed the door behind them.

The door slamming seemed to finally shake Sarah from her frozen state. She was facing the door and Michael, with her back to the chair where the growling was emanating from. Her voice was shaking as she managed to finally speak. The growling growing more intense behind her.

"M…M…M…Michael…"

Michael had moved right in front of her. He held up his right index finger to his lips indicating that he wanted her to stay silent. He placed his hands on her shoulders and began to move her to one side to get her out of harm's way so he could face the thing. It was at that moment they both heard the deep gravelly voice give its' command to Michael. Sarah was scared to death, she closed her eyes trying to pretend she was invisible.

"Leave the bitch where she is you fuck! I like the view."

He could hear it lick its lips and give a low gravelly perverted laugh. Michael was furious inside, but he knew he needed to control his anger, now more than ever. Michael spoke in a calm, clear, and matter-f-fact voice back to the demon.

"No."

He moved Sarah to his right so she was away from the wall towards the center of the room, with a clear shot to the exit door of the bedroom. It was at this moment he wished he had not slammed it shut so that Sarah could make a quicker exit when the time came. The growling came again. It began as if the demon was upset by Michael's actions, but then it turned into an almost cat like purr.

"You know Kenna, I like this view of the slut much better. I can see her ti…"

Michael cut the voice off.

"So what is it you want?"

Michael's eyes were adjusting better now to the darkness since he and Jeff had dropped their flashlights to help their friend. The only person still holding one was Sarah and hers was pointed at the floor. She stood still, stiff, frozen, her back to the middle of the room, starring at a side view of Michael while he stared at the young boy sitting in the recliner chair. Michael could see the boys' face, which was not his own anymore, and he could see that the boy, the creature that now inhabited the boys' body, was sitting crossed legged in the chair, it's arms resting on the arms of the chair. The face though, the face was drawn, almost pure white, the eyes sunken into the head, it looked like the face of a concentration camp victim. The body was thin and seemed weak, but Michael knew better. It was a stark contrast to the body of the young athletic boy that Michael had met three weeks earlier, but demonic possession takes its' toll on the human body and it does it quickly once full possession has taken place. Michael could see by the look on its' face it was annoyed with him, most likely for interrupting it.

"The same as we always want to dumb fuck!"
Remaining calm and asking obvious questions was a tactic Michael had learned long ago from his mentor, a Catholic priest, who was an exorcist, and had worked many cases throughout the world. It was a very useful and effective tactic against the demonic, because one thing he found demonic entities lacked was a tolerance for human stupidity. Demons are beings of high intelligence, they see themselves as being as far above humans as humans are above insects, but they are cruel beings, they hate humans, but they also love and lust for human feelings, emotions, and physical contact. We are their play things, at least that is how they see it, but they also hate us for being God's children and chosen. They hold great contempt for us and that is why they want us to suffer under them, they want God to suffer seeing his beloved children defiled and destroyed by them. This is what Michael learned to protect and fight against. This was his mission in life, to try and saved those dammed by demons and keep the demons at bay. Michael quipped back at the demon.

"Yes, but I just wanted to hear you to say it."
The creature shot back at him.

"FUCK YOU KENNA!"
Michael continued to speak calmly.

"I'm sorry, am I upsetting you? You know I don't want…"
The creature smiled at him and lowered its tone.

"So Kenna, have you fucked this new whore of yours yet? Has she swallowed your…"
Michael interrupted it again.

"Why do you do that? What's the point?"
The creature's face turned angry, but it still spoke in a lower tone.

"Because their all sluts and whores! All of them! But I bet this one's much better in the sack than that other dirty little high school slut we had last week. You know, the one whose pretty picture is on our wall."

The creature gave a big grin, extending its tongue and licking its lips. Michael knew the girl it was referring to. He chose not to imagine what it had done to her. His purpose right now was to try and gather information from the demon without it realizing it was giving him any. One thing the creature had given away was its obvious obsession with sex, more specifically sex with human females. This alone helped him narrow down the field of what demon he might be dealing with. Granted there are many, but not all are obsessed with sex as this one obviously was. It also saw human women as sexual objects, play things, and not as living, breathing, emotional beings. That helped him narrow the possibilities even more.

Michael glanced over at Sarah for just a quick moment, just to let her know he was still aware she was there, and he had not forgotten her. In that quick glance he could see the tears streaming from her beautiful green eyes which were now wide open, and that were now pleading with him to look at her, to save her from this nightmare, to get her away from this disgusting creature. Michael found himself looking back to Sarah, his emotions starting to get the better of him. The demon saw this.

"Aaaah Kenna. Don't tell me you have feelings for her. No, no, not just feelings, you love this whore don't you?"

Again, the big disgusting grin and then a low laugh that grew until it filled the entire house.

"Well if that's' the case I'll have to take her right here in front of you and see if you still love her then!"

The demon also knew the game, they always did. They always knew the moves on the chess board before the game was even begun. That was their advantage, they could see the game before it ever even happened, but the one thing even they could not foresee was the game's outcome. Human free will and our ability to change our minds at a moment's notice prevent them from foretelling the future, but by knowing the game they could try to manipulate it to their advantage.

"If you touch her so help me God I'll..."

Michael's thought was interrupted by the sound of his walkie crackling to life. It was Beth.

"Michael, are you ok?! Michael answer me!"

Michael grabbed the walkie from his belt.

"Not now Beth."

Beth insisted.

"Michael, you need to know this. Abby and I have been through the whole house. Even Mrs. Casey helped. We've found nothing. I repeat, *Nothing*! There's only one room we haven't checked Michael. Just one room! Do you understand!?"

Michael was silent for a moment. His eyes glanced around the room.

"Yes, I understand."

And he did, but the problem was he did not see anything in the room that seemed old enough or even just stood out as something that would have a demonic attachment, or be a portal for one, but then again, he could not see behind him and he dare not turn his back on the creature. It was at that moment that he felt something grab his hand. It startled him and he jumped.

He looked down and saw Sarah was grasping his right hand. He felt awful. He had allowed her to be put into this situation, one he really knew she was not prepared for, one he knew was going to be dangerous. He slowly raised his gaze to meet hers. He could still see the tears running down her cheeks, but as he looked into her eyes he noticed she was no longer crying. The fear had gone from her face. She squeezed his hand tighter and glanced towards the wall behind them.

"Awwwww, holding hands, how sweet. Is it as sweet as her...."

Sarah turned and glared at the creature.

"SHUT UP YOU SICK ABOMINATION!!!"

The creatures face contorted, its' grin turning into a scowl. It lashed out and had the framed photos and posters on the walls fly at Sarah, smacking her in the head and upper body. Michael grabbed her and pulled her into him, shielding her with his own body, and during the course of doing that spun them both so he could look at the wall that had been behind him, the one Sarah had indicated towards through her eye movement. He saw it. There on the wall, larger than life, the same wall Robert had been pinned to. How did he miss it! How could he not have seen it! The huge antique mirror! The same one Sarah, Jeff and Robert had all spotted when first searching the room.

This was it. This was how the demon entered the home. How it came to possess the young boy Jeremy. This same demon he had fought before somehow found its' way to the portal in that mirror and into this home.

Items in the room kept flying at them, hitting them. Michael could now feel that Sarah's body had gone limp in his arms. There was blood in her hair. She was unconscious. Michael hung onto her but he knew he would need to let go. He knew what he had to do to save both her and the boy.

"HOW DID YOU GET INTO THIS HOME?!"

Michael screamed at the creature over the clattering and banging of flying objects. Then he heard a loud screeching/scraping noise and looked to the direction it was coming from. The large dresser was moving quickly across the room at him and Sarah. He took advantage of the moment and flung them both towards the door to the room. He hung tightly onto Sarah as he rolled them together across the floor, the dresser slamming down, and shattering on the floor where they had been. Michael was not quite quick enough though. The dresser smashed down onto his right ankle, breaking it. He winced from the pain, but kept to his plan. He still had his walkie in his left hand and used it to call Beth and Abby.

"BETH! GET UP HERE I NEED YOU NOW!"

There was no reply, but he could hear the sounds of heavy, fast footsteps running up the marble staircase and down the hallway to the room. More than one person was coming to their aid. Just as one of his people was opening the door, it was slammed shut by an unseen force. Michael could hear Jeff yelling on the other side.

"What the fuck!"

Then rhythmic banging as Jeff tried to break it down. For just an instant Michael felt a wave of relief rush over him knowing that Jeff had kept his word and come back to the house as promised. It was a fleeting moment though as more things were flung at Michael, this time targeting his broken ankle. A heavy picture frame struck it square on, and Michael cried out from the searing pain. Jeff and Beth yelled out to him, he could hear Abby and Mrs. Casey crying, Mrs. Casey calling for Jeremy. The demon heard her as well and laughingly taunted her.

"JEREMY'S SOUL BURNS IN HELL! YOUR SON BURNS IN HELL! HAHAHAHAHAHA!!!!!"

Enough was enough; Michael had to do something to distract the creature. If he could just reach one of his cases they had brought into the room with them, he could get to some holy water. The nearest case was three feet away, and if he moved to get it the creature would see and stop him or perhaps turn its attack again to Sarah. He realized he had one thing still in his possession he could use, and it was otherwise useless to him now anyway. He switched the walkie to his right hand, sat up and threw it with all his might at the creature whom was still seated in the chair about eighteen feet away. The walkie flew across the room, but the creature never saw it, or even sensed it. The demon had its eyes closed and was too focused on its own pleasure of tormenting Michael, his crew and the family. That was a mistake. It struck Jeremy in his right temple with enough force that it knocked the boy unconscious, and the creature along with him. At that moment everything went silent, and the demonic laughing and taunting stopped. Michael knew there had to have been some kind of divine intervention in his throw, because that was just an impossible feat from where he was and the pain he was in. He also knew the silence would not last long, he had perhaps only moments before the boy came to.

Jeff had still been bashing at the door and another hit came just as everything fell silent. Jeff went flying through the now unobstructed door and fell across the room. He recovered quickly and went to Michael. Beth ran in behind him. Michael waved her off.

"Don't let Mrs. Casey in here!"

Without a word Beth turned and went back out. Michael could hear Beth restraining Mrs. Casey, the woman crying and demanding to see her son. Michael looked up at Jeff. He rolled himself off of Sarah.

"Jeff, get her out of here. Please, take care of her."

Sarah was just beginning to wake, but she was still dazed and her mind was blurry. Jeff took her under the arm, got her to her feet, and got her out of the room. This time there was no looking back, no nod of acknowledgement. Jeff knew what he had to do, but he had expected to hand Sarah over to Beth and Abby and go back in to help Michael, but that did not happen. Michael had plans of his own.

As Jeff went out the doorway with Sarah, He had not seen that Michael had managed to stand up, and support himself on his one good leg. He was right behind them as they exited the room, but

Michael did not follow. He quietly and slowly closed the door behind them. Jeff did not realize it until he heard the door latch behind them as they entered into the hallway.

"Abby, take Sarah!"

Jeff handed the girl over to Abby, who was not quite strong enough to hold her up on her own, and had to set her down against the far wall of the hallway.

"Michael! Open the door! Michael!"

Jeff cried out to his friend while banging on the door but Michael did not respond.

Michael could hear his friend plead for him to not do this and to let him in, let him help him with this, but Michael was not willing to put anyone else at risk anymore. This was between him and the creature, the demon that possessed this young teenage boy. The key to ending this was the large antique mirror mounted on the boys' bedroom wall. Michael hobbled his way over to it, wincing from the knife like pain that shot through his ankle as he made his way to the wall to help support himself. When he reached the wall he placed both hands on it, as if preparing to be arrested. He did this in order to best support himself and keep his weight off his right leg. He stopped for a moment and listened. Jeff was still banging at the door and pleading with him to let him in, but that was not what he was listening for.

"Jeff, stop!"

Michael spoke in a loud but whispered voice.

"For God sake please stop. I'm not letting anyone else in here and you're not helping. Back away. Please my friend. Please back away."

The banging and yelling stopped.

"Michael..."

There was hesitation and sadness in Jeff's voice.

"I'm...I'm sorry...I..."

Michael leaned his forehead on the wall in front of him and closed his eyes. He loved his friend like a brother. There was nothing they would not do for each other. That went for Robert as well.

"Never mind that now. It's ok my brother."

Michael did not want his friend and colleague to think he was upset with him, he was not. He just needed him to keep control of things on the other side of the door.

"Jeff, just do me a favor and get everyone downstairs. Make sure Sarah and the others are all safe, you as well. How's Sarah doing? How's Mrs. Casey?"

Jeff spoke softly.

"Beth already moved Mrs. Casey and Abby down in to the sitting room. Sarah is here in the hallway with me sitting against the far wall. She's still pretty out of it Michael."

Michael lifted his head and looked into the darkness of the room toward the direction of his friends' voice.

"How about Robert? Is he ok?"

The two men were still speaking in whispered tones.

"Yeah, Robert's going to be ok. Livy and I took him to the hospital like you said. She stayed there with him and I came back like I said I would. He was conscious and trying to talk when I left him there with Livy. She got a doctor to look at him right away. I think he's going to have a really bad sore throat for a while though."

Jeff smiled to himself hoping that perhaps he made Michael smile or at least broke some of the tension in that room. Then Jeff got serious again.

"You and I both know it's going to take him some time to recover psychologically from it, but in the end he'll be ok."

Michael did smile and looked up into the darkness toward the ceiling, toward heaven. He was glad Jeff had Livy go with Robert to the hospital. That girl would take no BS from anyone when it came to her friends and family. He said a short prayer and then blessed himself.

"Good, good. That's good. Thank you Jeff."

Jeff could hear that his friend was in pain and his breathing was a bit labored.

"Michael, is there anything I can do for you? Anything I can get you?"

Michael turned his head to look at the large mirror hanging on the wall.

"No Jeff. I'm ok."

Both men knew that was a lie.

"I have what I need now and I know what has to be done."

Michael did know what he needed to do, but the bigger problem, the piece of the puzzle he did not have yet, was how to get it done. This was not something you did by brute force. It is a game of wits, of faith, and it always has a winner and a looser.

"The best way you can help me now is by taking care of the others, ok?"

Jeff was leaning against the door with both hands on it, his own forehead pressed against it, as if trying to melt his way through it somehow.

"Ok Michael. Consider it done."

With that Jeff pushed himself away from the door and set his attention to Sarah, who was still slumped up against the wall where Abby had set her down. Jeff kneeled down next to her and took her pulse; it was steady and strong as was her breathing. If it were not for the contusion and blood on her head, he would have thought she was just taking a nap in the hallway.

"Come on Sarah, we need to get you up and out of here. Let's get you moving sister."

Sarah was half conscious now. She recognized Jeff's voice and looked up at him. She was still dazed and slightly confused but she remembered most of what was happening, what had happened.

"Jeff…"

Her voice was quiet, weak, and bit strained.

"Wh…Where's Michael?"

There was no way Jeff was going to tell her the truth.

"Don't worry about him, he's ok."

Another lie, but he had to get Sarah down stairs and out of that hallway before all hell broke loose again inside that room.

"But…where is he?"

Her voice was shaky and filled with concern.

"He's…he's down in the sitting room with the others. He injured his ankle that's why I'm taking care of you."

Sarah put her hand to her forehead. She felt dizzy. She could feel her hair was wet but did not give it much thought. Her thoughts were to Michael.

"Ok…let's go then, I want to see him. I need to see Michael."

Jeff got her to the staircase and they slowly began making their way down to the first floor.

"Let me help you up and we'll go see him together."

Jeff hated lying, but this was for his friend, to keep the promise he made to keep Sarah safe. He knew Sarah would be pissed once she knew the truth, but he would deal with that once he got her downstairs in the sitting room with the others."

Michael could hear his friend talking to Sarah in the hallway and could hear Sarah responding; that made him feel a lot better, knowing that she was at least semi-conscious and still alive. He could hear Jeff getting her to her feet and then helping her down the hallway to the stairs, it made him feel even better knowing she would be out of harms' way. He turned his attention back to the room, listening for anything that might indicate the boy was waking up. He did notice the change in the atmosphere of the room. The awful rotting smell was gone, the room had gotten warmer, and the darkness was not as dark as before, all signs that the demon was not present, at least not at the moment, and that there had also been some kind of angelic intercession. Again, he knew it would not last long though. It was just a matter of time, perhaps just moments, before the boy awoke and the creature returned…with a vengeance. Even though he had asked the demon what it wanted, he already knew, it was in the message of the EVP. It wanted Michael's soul, it wanted to possess him, get him out of the way, kill the exorcist, kill the enemy of the demonic. It was just using the boy to get to him, but it would take Jeremy's soul too if it could. It already had the boy's body so taking his soul was just the next step in the process. All the demon had to do was get Jeremy to kill himself which Michael knew it could do anytime it had wanted to over the past two to three weeks, but it had not, that is why Michael knew what it really wanted was him.

Still the room was silent at the moment but time was limited. Michael did not have time to dwell on what the creature wanted, he had to focus and develop a plan to trick it, to send it back to where it came from, and save both the boy and himself if possible. Michael put his forehead against the wall again.

"Think, think. The mirror is the answer. You have to get it to go back into the mirror, then seal the portal. You'll need holy water to seal the mirror with, where are the cases?"

Michael turned slowly around, his back now to the wall, and looked about the room. One of the two cases they had brought with them was ten feet away in the middle of the room, the other he could not see anywhere, but there was debris strewn all over the room now. He glanced about the room. On the floor, just to his left, were the two flashlights, still on, that he and Jeff had dropped when trying to help Robert. Then he spotted it, just barely lit by one of the lights, he could see part of the second case just two feet from him, under some of the remains of the dresser. It was painful but he lowered himself to the floor and reached for the case.

Michael was able to get his hand on one corner of the case and pulled it to him dragging the flashlights in front of it. He grabbed one of the lights, stuck it between his teeth and then used both hands to unlatch the case and open it. Everything inside was still in one piece, he found the bottle of holy water and also his Saint Benedict Crucifix which had been blessed by the Holy Father himself years ago when Michael met him as a young teenager at World Youth Day. This blessed crucifix and prayer to the dear Saint Benedict would be key to exercising this demon.

"Thank you dear God."

Michael whispered as he could feel the anxiety, stress and even the pain leave his body as he held the crucifix in his hands. He spat out the flashlight, closed his eyes and began to pray the novena to Saint Benedict.

"Glorious St. Benedict, sublime model of virtue, pure vessel of God's grace! Behold me humbly kneeling at your feet. I implore you in your loving kindness to pray for me before the throne of God. To you I have recourse in the dangers that daily surround me. Shield me against my selfishness and my indifference to God and to my neighbor. Inspire me to imitate you in all things. May your blessing be with me always, so that I may see and serve Christ in others and work for His kingdom.

Graciously obtain for me from God those favors and graces which I need so much in the trials, miseries and afflictions of life. Your heart was always full of love, compassion and mercy toward those who were afflicted or troubled in any way. You never dismissed without consolation and assistance anyone who had recourse to you. I therefore invoke your powerful intercession, confident in the hope that you will hear my prayer and obtain for me the special grace and favor I earnestly implore help me in your name and in the name of Jesus Christ to exercise this demon from this boy, this innocent member of Christ's flock. Help me, great St. Benedict, to live and die as a faithful child of God, to run in the sweetness of His loving will and to attain the eternal happiness of heaven.
- Amen."

He felt the darkness close in around him, the room grew ice cold again, and the stench of a rotting corpse returned again as he prayed. He heard the tormented growling begin again and grow louder. He heard the heavy foot falls moving towards him from across the room, until they were on top of him. He could smell and feel the hot stinking breath of the creature in his face. Michael finished his prayer and opened his eyes to face the evil thing; but not for himself, not for his own glory, but for the glory of God and to fight for the soul of Christ's poor lost lamb, to fight for the soul of the boy. To fight for Jeremy.

Sarah sat hunched over on the huge sectional sofa, her head in her hands. Beth sat next to her holding an ice pack on the back of her head where she had been struck by a heavy object, most likely one of their own two cases that they had brought into the boys' bedroom. The bleeding had stopped, but she had a terrible headache and the anger she now felt towards Jeff for lying to her about Michael was not helping it any.

"Why the hell did you leave him up there all alone Jeff?! Why?!"
Jeff knew she was angry at him, he had expected it, he knew she was not going to accepting anything he told her, as all rational thinking went out the door when love was involved. He knew she was in love with Michael, but he felt he at least owed it to her to try and explain.

"Sarah, when I pulled you out of the room he locked the door behind all of us before I could go back for him. I did not plan it this. I had no intention of…"
Sarah was not having any of it.

"Bullshit!"
She lifted her head to look at Jeff. She saw the sincerity in his eyes, the sadness. She was still angry, but she knew the three men were like brothers. They had founded the team together years ago. They had been through everything together. She knew it was not his fault. She knew in her heart that it had been Michael that planned to lock the door and face the beast alone, not Jeff, she also knew that Jeff was probably just as upset as she was with Michael and just as concerned for him.

"I'm sorry Jeff."
Her voice lowered.

"I know you would never leave him unless he gave you no other choice."

Jeff knelt down on the floor in front of her and looked into her eyes.

"Sarah, he asked me to…"

Sarah cut him off. She put her hand on his shoulder.

"I know what he asked you Jeff."

She did, even though she never heard their conversation, she knew what Michael had asked of his friend.

"This is all my fault, all my fault."

Sarah lowered her head again and put her hand over her face in shame. Jeff swung his body up and sat on the other side of Sarah from Beth.

"No, don't say that. It's not your fault."

Beth piped in with Jeff, not totally believing her own words perhaps, but there was no point in blaming anyone at this stage of the game.

"Jeff's right Sarah. It's not your fault. It's no one's fault but that thing up there."

Beth's words ripped through Mrs. Casey like a dull saw blade. She tore into Beth.

"WHAT DO YOU MEAN THING?!"

Mrs. Casey was sitting at the far end of sectional with Abby.

"THAT THING AS YOU CALL IT IS MY SON!"

Jeff was trying to keep everyone's emotions in check or at least under some kind of control.

"Calm down Mrs. Casey, Beth didn't mean…"

Mrs. Casey cut him off.

"YES SHE DID! SHE SEES MY SON AS A MONSTER! HE IS NOT A MONSTER! HE'S NOT!"

She broke down and began crying uncontrollably. Abby tried to comfort her but Alice Casey pushed her away. Jeff, put his hand on Sarah's shoulder, gave her a pat and went to Alice.

"Mrs. Casey…Alice…No one here thinks your son is a monster. He's not. The thing that possesses him is the monster. That's what Beth was referring to, not your son, not Jeremy."

He spoke softly to her, trying to be reassuring. He looked back at Beth and gave her that look of *Think before you speak*. Mrs. Casey was still crying, there was no stopping it, she had to get it out, and everyone in the room knew that. All they could do was try to comfort her. The fate of her son and his soul was now in the hands of just one of man, and that one man was injured and beaten, and hardly in any condition to even protect or help himself, let alone a boy possessed by a demon from hell. Sarah looked up at Jeff and then to the other team members.

"So what do we do now? What's our next step? What's the plan?" Jeff was stoic in his reply. Beth and Abby said nothing.

"We wait like Michael asked."

Sarah took Beth's silence as an agreement with Jeff's statement, and she could see by the look in Abby's eyes that the girl was just frightened and probably just wanted to go home and forget all this ever happened.

"Well, you all do what you want. I'm going back up there to help Michael whether he wants me to or not."

Jeff could see that Sarah was resolute in her decision, but he had to try and stop her, he owed it to Michael to keep his promise to keep her safe.

"Sarah, I can't let you do that."

Sarah stood up from the sofa, she was determined to go back upstairs.

"Try and stop me!"

Jeff knew there was no reasoning with her, he had to try and make it clear to her that she was not ready for this, that going back up there would just put her and Michael back in danger again.

"Sarah, you froze up there! We both did! It almost cost Michael and Robert their lives!"

Sarah's face turned red with anger and frustration, not with Jeff but with herself for her own failings in that room.

"What?! You don't think I know that?! You don't think I know what I did?! The problems I caused!"

The tension, frustration and anger that both of them felt just exploded.

"Not just you Sarah! Both of us! We were both in that damn room! We both froze up! We both made mistakes!"

Sarah glared back at him.

"And I won't make those same mistakes again Jeff! I know what to expect now! That demon, that boy, doesn't scare me anymore!"

Jeff cold hear the conviction in her voice and saw it in her face, but he knew she was wrong, and still did not totally understand what they were dealing with.

"I can see that Sarah, and that's my point! That's your next big mistake! Because you should be sacred of what's up there! Don't you get it!? It doesn't want you to be afraid of it! It wants you to be accepting of it! It wants you to get close to it! That's how it takes you! That's how it gains possession of you!"

Sarah was still determined to make her point.

"But Michael...!"

Jeff had enough, he cut her off in mid-sentence.

"Sarah! Don't say it because it's not true!"

Jeff took a deep breath to compose himself, them yelling at each other was not helping anyone, especially not Michael who was up in that room alone with the demon. Neither of them was listening to each other, they were both angry but not with each other, they were angry with Michael for locking them out of the room, for not allowing them to help him, for putting himself in danger. Jeff spoke calmly now o Sarah.

"Sarah, please, believe me when I tell you that Michael is probably more afraid of that demon than any of us, and with good reason. He knows exactly what that thing is and what it's capable of. Just because he doesn't show his fear doesn't mean he doesn't have any. He just knows better than any of us how to control it."

Sarah took a deep breath as well, she suddenly felt a bit dizzy and sat back down on the sofa. She looked up at Jeff, still defiant as ever, but she too so no point in continuing to yell at him when it was not him she was angry with.

"That may be the case Jeff..."

He cut her off again.

"It is."

Which just served to piss her off and make her more determined than ever.

"Whatever! It doesn't matter! I'm going back up there. I'm not leaving him to face that demon all alone. I love him Jeff. I love Michael and I can't, I won't, abandon him."

It was now obvious to Jeff that he was not going to change her mind, talk her out of it, or stop her.

"It seems you've made up your mind then."

Sarah look directly into his eyes.

"Yes Jeff, I have."

Jeff held his hand out to her, offering to help her up from the sofa.

"Well if I can't change your mind, then I'm going to have to go with you."

Sarah took it.

"You don't have to do that Jeff. I can't ask that of you."

He pulled her up from the sofa.

"First…Yes I do. Second, I already made a promise to that man upstairs that I would look after you and make sure you're safe, so you see I have to go with you."

Jeff turned his attention to Beth and Abby.

"You ladies stay here and take care of Mrs. Casey she's going to need you both to get through this. Abby, I know you're afraid but we need you, and you're safe down here. Please just stay with Beth and do as she asks ok."

Abby nodded and managed a whispered "Yes. Ok." in response. Sarah looked at Beth, leaned forward, and put her hand on Beth's knee.

"Thanks for the ice pack and for taking care of me Beth."

Beth nodded and put her hand on Sarah's and smiled at her.

"Anytime Sarah."

Sarah and Jeff headed for the staircase, but Beth stopped them.

"One thing you two, before you head back up there."

The look on Beth's face became serious and concerned.

"I can sense that this is almost at an end. It won't be long now. I can't tell you what's going to happen, or how, or exactly when, but I can feel that it's nearly over. It's going to get bad, very bad, perhaps more on a spiritual level than a physical I'm not sure, but more than anything else right now, we need to focus on Michael and Jeremy and pray for them. Pray to the angels to help them both. I know that sounds hokey to some of you, but I'm serious and I truly believe that our prayers will be heard and will help them."

Jeff and Sarah looked at her. Beth knew that Jeff believed but she was not so sure about Sarah. She knew Sarah was a woman with her roots firm in the ground. She accepted the belief in spiritualism and angels and God, but was not necessarily a believer herself. Sarah responded to her first.

"Beth. Honey I've been praying all night and I'm not about to stop now."

Jeff verbalized Sarah's sentiment in a single word.

"Ditto."

Black as pitch but gleaming like two pools of water in moonlight, the boys' eyes seemed like huge black saucers only inches from Michael's face. The eyes seemed almost lifeless though, sunken into the skeletal like sockets of the boys' skull. Michael knew better though, these were not the eyes of the boy, but of the creature that possessed him, they were the eyes of the demon. Michael stared deeply back into them.

"So what do you see demon? What do you see in my eyes?"

The prayer and his faith had brought new life and strength to Michael. His mind was clear and sharp. He was ready to match wits with the thing and through his faith and strength of God, exorcise this demon from the boy and bring this possession to an end.

"I see your fear!"

The creature contorted its head first right and then left, but never blinking or removing its' gaze from Michael.

"My fear? Are you sure demon? Are you sure that's what you see, or is it something else?"

The demon was right about one thing, Michael was afraid and while he did have a good healthy fear of this creature, that was not the fear that was first and foremost in him. It was the fear of failing, of failing to save the boy, of failing God, but for now he had pushed those fears deep into the darkness of his own mind. What the demon perceived as fear in Michael's eyes was actually empathy and determination. Empathy for this poor creature whose endless existence was filled with nothing but pain, loneliness and servitude to a master that was nothing more than pure evil, an evil older than the universe itself. Empathy also for the boy whom it possessed, tortured and tormented, and finally determination to bring this all to an end. Michael knew the demon was wrong about what he saw in his eyes, but he was not going to tell it that.

"Aaaahhh hisssss....Yessss. Fear."

The demon was trying to look confident, but Michael could see the doubt in its expression.

"Very well then."

Michael was quick to quip back.

"Do you want to know what I see in your eyes demon?"

The creature was squatting down on all fours in front of him, smiling at him. But its' expression changed at this question and it backed away from him about foot. The creature seemed puzzled and annoyed. Doubt crept into its thoughts. Perhaps it had read Michael wrong, maybe he was not afraid. It thought quickly and tried to change the topic of their discussion.

"Why do you call me that?!"

The demon scowled at Michael.

"Call you what?"

Michael only asked to annoy it. The creature was not pleased with Michael's feigned ignorance. It yelled at him.

"That!"

Michael shot back again, this time he smiled at the creature. He knew that would only antagonize it more, but that's what he was trying to do.

"That what?"

The creature was angry, it lunged toward Michael, stopping again just inches from his him, face to face once again.

"That name!"

Michael did not flinch, he looked deep into its dark black eyes. He spoke slowly and clearly so the demon would hear him.

"What name?"

The creature hissed and growled back at him.

"You know what you called me!!!"

It seemed as though the whole room began to shake. Michael knew he was getting to the creature. It was getting angry with him. He was slowly turning the tables, if he could keep it up he could get it to make a mistake and he would have the advantage for the first time.

"So let me tell you what I see in your eyes demon."

Michael was calm and relaxed in his tone.

"STOP CALLING ME THAT YOU FUCKING…!!!!"

Michael shot back quickly, cutting the demon off, hoping to push it over the edge to make a mistake and give Michael what he needed. He screamed into the creatures face.

"THEN WHAT SHOULD I CALL YOU!!!"

In its fit of anger, the creature finally betrayed its own name to Michael.

"AZAJMES!!!"

Michael sat there, his back to the wall. At first his expression was blank, he was thinking, his mind racing to find the reference, the name, but he knew the response had not been straight forward. It would never be straight forward. Just like in the EVP, it would be said in reverse. Then it clicked in his mind, and Michael began to smile. The creatures grimace faded from its face with the realization of what it had just done. It began to slowly back away from Michael. Then Michael began to speak, quoting a passage from the Book of Enoch.

"And it came to pass when the children of men had multiplied that in those days were born unto them beautiful and comely daughters. And the angels, the children of the heaven, saw and lusted after them, and said to one another: 'Come, let us choose us wives from among the children of men and beget us children.' And "Semjaza", who was their leader, said unto them: 'I fear ye will not indeed agree to do this deed, and I alone shall have to pay the penalty of a great sin.' And they all answered him and said: 'Let us all swear an oath, and all bind ourselves by mutual imprecations not to abandon this plan but to do this thing.' Then swore they all together and bound themselves by mutual imprecations upon it. And they were in all two hundred; who descended in the days of Jared on the summit of Mount Hermon, and they called it Mount Hermon, because they had sworn and bound themselves by mutual imprecations upon it..."

"I know your name. You gave me your name! You freely gave me your name and with that the power to command you! That same power that was given by God to King Solomon, I now have over you through your own capitulation!"

Michael was now standing, his back still against the wall to support his weight. He had slid himself up the wall, pushing himself up with his one good leg and his arms. The demon was still squatting on all fours in front of him but had backed away towards the corner and the recliner chair, like a trapped animal. Michael held up the crucifix. The demon knew he could not allow Michael to speak its name, if Michael did he would have power over him. The demon locked its' gaze on the huge mirror behind Michael. Michael began to speak again.

"Semj..."

Michael was struck hard from behind by the huge mirror that had hung on the wall. It knocked him to the floor. His full weight went on to his right leg and he felt and heard a loud SNAP followed by excruciating pain and then...nothing. Michael blacked out.

Sarah and Jeff were still on the staircase when they heard the voices coming from the room, but they could not tell what was being said. Then they could hear the creature screaming and then Michael screaming back. As they moved down the hallway they could hear Michael talking calmly again, it sounded almost like a prayer or as if he was quoting something, then growling followed by loud crashing and banging and a huge thud as something or someone fell hard to the floor. The two of them began to run down the hall to the door, Sarah yelling to Michael, then there was another loud crash and the sound of shattering glass from the room. Jeff literally hit the door first, but it did not give, although the crack in the door did widen. Jeff saw this and began a relentless attack on it, driving into with his shoulder again and again, then stepping back and kicking with all his might into the oak door. Finally, it began to give way. Sarah was still yelling for Michael but he did not respond.

The creature could see that Michael was not moving so it crawled back over to him. The large mirror that had been on the wall was laying part way on top of him. The creature reached over and grabbed the nearest corner of it, and picked it up about a foot off of Michael. It looked under it. The mirror was cracked but not shattered. The thing lifted it up higher, stretching its arm above its head as high as it could while still squatting over Michael. Then, with all its inhuman strength it slammed it down on top of Michael again. This time the mirror shattered into pieces, some of them slicing into Michael's back, shoulders and face. The portal through which it had come was destroyed; even if Michael did wake up he would not be able to exile it that way. Then the demon heard Sarah's voice and the sound of people running down the hallway, followed by the pounding on the door of someone trying to force their way in. The creature realized its' time was up. The human body it now possessed was tired from the long nights battle it had put it through, it could feel the boys heart pounding, almost bursting from its' chest. It could not take much more and there would be more once those two broke through the door. Also the sun was starting to rise, the night was almost over, and the door was giving way to the relentless pounding it was taking. If his friends rescued him, then Michael would surely come back and expel him from the boy, as the demon knew it had erred in giving Michael its name. No, the demon could not allow that to happen, he could not allow Michael to win and save both their souls. He could only take one soul now, he had to choose and choose quickly. But which would do more damage. Which would cause more grief and perhaps, just perhaps, provide more souls to burn in the fires of hell? The creature stood up and walked towards the far right wall where the balcony was. It stopped in front of the sliding glass door and stared at its' reflection in the glass, its eyes changed from the glossy pitch black back to a bright blue, as the creature allowed the boy Jeremy to surface from his tormented mind. For the first time in weeks Jeremy, the boy, could see himself for how he really looked, and he could remember all of the things the demon had done to him and to others he cared about and loved. He remembered the horrific things he had done to his young friend from school, the disgusting things the demon had forced the poor girl to do for its' own pleasure. It was more than his mind could bear. He saw in himself the ANIMAL, the MONSTER he had let himself become to gain the favors of the demon he had thought could give him all that he wanted in life.

Sarah could hear what sounded like weeping coming from the room. At first she thought it sounded like a young girl, but she quickly realized it was a young boy, it was Jeremy! The boy himself was back! Her mind raced, maybe Michael had been successful, maybe he had driven the demon out! She began to relax a bit thinking everything was finally going to be ok. Finally, the door gave way, it split completely in two. The latch half falling to the floor and the other half swinging wide open under Jeff's final shoulder ram. Jeff flew into the room but kept his footing, Sarah followed right behind him. The room was beginning to brighten as the sun rose outside, the soft orange glow to the east coming through the open balcony door. From that moment on everything seemed to move in slow motion to Sarah. She saw Jeff frantically swing his head to the left spotting Michael on the floor, covered in blood, Michael was half conscious now and pointing towards the balcony. He spoke one word, "Jeremy" and Jeff swung his attention to where Michael was pointing. There, standing poised on the rail of the balcony, twenty-five feet above the pavement of the huge circular driveway in front of the house, was Jeremy with his back to all of them. Sarah heard Jeff yell the boys' name as he ran towards him. She saw the boy glance back for just a moment before allowing himself to fall from the rail,

Jeff missed catching the boy by his ankle by only inches. Jeff watched in horror as young Jeremy hit the pavement below head first, shattering his skull and neck. Jeff fell slumped over the railing, crying and repeating "No, No, No…" over and over. Sarah knew there was nothing she could do for the poor boy now except cry and pray for his soul. She turned her attention to Michael and knelt by him putting his head in her lap. He was bleeding terribly. She could see that his right ankle was completely shattered and shards of mirror were stuck into him like porcupine quills. She realized she still had her own walkie on her, she took it from her coat pocket and called down to Beth. Time sped up again…

"Beth this is Sarah!"

Beth could hear the urgency in Sarah's voice. Downstairs they had all heard the yelling and loud thud come from outside but had no idea what was going on.

"I hear you Sarah, what's going on!? Is everything…everyone ok!?"

Beth's voice was shaky. Beth's anxiety was obvious to Sarah by the sound of her voice, Sarah's first concerns now though were Mrs. Casey and Michael.

"Is Mrs. Casey there with you?"

Sarah needed to know, she need to make sure Mrs. Casey did not go outside, at least not until the police and ambulance arrived, and she needed to have someone take care of making that call as well.

"No. Right now she's in the kitchen with Abby. Sarah, we all just heard this loud noise from outside in the driveway. What was it? Should I check on it?"

Beth was worried that something terrible might have just happened, Sarah confirmed her fear for her.

"Beth, keep Mrs. Casey in the house. Don't let her go outside. You can't let her leave the house. Her son…Jeremy…"

The emotions were welling up inside her, she choked them back down.

"There's been an accident. We need the police and an ambulance immediately! Michael is hurt badly and Jeremy…Jeremy is…he's…"

Sarah could not bring herself to say the words. She was not even sure what to really say, she kept it short and to the point.

"…he jumped head first from his balcony."

There was silence on the other end.

"Beth did you hear me!?"

Beth did not know what to say, although she knew what she had to do.

"Yes, I heard you."

Beth's tone was quiet and subdued. Sarah was still scared and filled with anxiety, but her mind was sharp and focused, and she was in charge of the situation. That's the thing about fear. You never know how you are going to react to it until you do. It can either make you freeze in place or it can bring you almost super human clarity and focus to be able to handle whatever is feeding your fear. This time it brought Sarah the clarity and focus she needed to handle the situation.

"Call the ambulance now and keep everyone inside ok?!"

The confidence and calm in Sarah's voice snapped Beth back and into action.

"Yes. Ok. I'm on it."

Sarah tossed the walkie to the floor.

Moments seemed like hours as Sarah sat with the now unconscious Michael, while Jeff had gone back down stairs to wait for the ambulance and police with Beth, and Abby stayed in the kitchen with Mrs. Casey. The sound of the ambulance and police sirens brought with them a wave of relief that settled over Sarah. She put her head down against Michaels' and began to cry.

A week later Sarah found herself back at the hospital where the two ambulance had taken her, Michael, Jeremy, and Mrs. Casey that night. She knew where she was going as she had gone to visit Michael every day since it all took place. She walked straight into the room and to Michael's bed. Jeff and Robert were both already there. They both smiled when they saw her enter the room, she smiled back at them.

"Well good evening boys."

Jeff and Robert responded together.

"Good evening Sarah."

She actually had not seen Robert since that night, but she kept tabs on him through Jeff and Olivia.

"Sounds like you pretty much have your voice back Robert. How do you feel?"

Sarah still felt bad for not moving to help him that night.

"Well young miss, I feel a lot better than your man here does."
Robert smiled and nodded to Michael who was laying in the hospital
bed.

"Yeah, well at least I don't sound like a rusty stove pipe."
Michael quipped and smiled at his friends.

"So how's my lady doing tonight? Oh, and by the way, with all of
  you here can someone please tell me who's minding the store?"
Sarah gave him a look and shook her head, and then nudged him
over so she could sit on the bed next to him.

"Well I'm doing just fine thank you my dear."
She leaned over and kissed him.

"As for whom is minding the store that would be Beth."
Michael looked up at her in surprise.

"Are you serious!? I thought Beth and Abby decided to call it quits
  after that night?"
Sarah stroked her fingers through his thick auburn hair.

"They did. But Beth came back yesterday. She said she couldn't let
  the evil that's out there stop her from doing what she loves, or
  from trying to help others."
Michael look around the room at his friends. He smiled. He was
proud of Beth's decision and her strength and commitment.

"She's right about that."
His friends all nodded in agreement. Sarah sat for a moment just
looking deep into Michael's eyes; Jeff and Robert noticed and took
the hint.

"Okay, Robert and I are out of here. We've wasted enough of this
  guy's time and we need to get back and give Beth a hand."
Michael looked up at his friend.

"Jeff, I know I haven't said it yet, and I know you would say I
  don't need to but, thank you for keeping Sarah safe that night, for
  keeping them all safe."
Jeff smiled softly, but then hung his head.

"Yeah…well…I didn't keep them all safe did I."
Michael knew what he was referring to.

"Jeff, you took care of everyone I asked you to. Jeremy was *my*
  responsibility, not yours. You understand?"
Jeff nodded and looked back up at his friend.

"Yeah, I do, but that doesn't make it any easier. We're a team you
  know. We all win or lose together."

Michael felt for his friend. He knew Jeff felt responsible for Jeremy.

"Yeah, but that call was on me."

Jeff nodded to Michael and gave another quick smile, and reached up and wiped his eyes. Michael and Sarah could both see that he had teared up. Robert put his hand on his friends back.

"Come on Jeff we need to get going."

Jeff looked to Robert, then turned his attention back to Michael.

"Yeah, okay. Oh Michael, one last thing. Olivia said she would be over later to see you as well, before she heads over to the office."

Michael nodded; he was glad to know Olivia was sticking around as well, but he was not surprised, she was a strong and determined young lady; then Jeff and Robert turned and left the room together. Michael turned back to Sarah who was still starring at him.

"What's on your mind?"

Michael could see something was bothering her. Sarah gave a deep sigh.

"I hadn't wanted to bother you with this yet because of what you've been through yourself, but…Mrs. Casey…Alice…she attempted to kill herself two nights ago."

Michael did not say anything, he just seemed to be waiting for her to finish talking, but Sarah could tell he was choking back his emotions.

"It's ok Michael. Alice is ok. Her husband and daughter returned home and found her before it was too late. She tried to overdose on sleeping pills, but they got her to the hospital in time. She's actually up on the seventh floor right now getting the help she needs to deal with losing Jeremy."

Michael remained silent for a moment.

"I'm glad they got to her in time. I just hope she and her family can recover from this. I'll ask Father Carlos from their church to check in on her later."

Michael could see something else was also on Sarah's mind.

"Something else is bothering you, what is it?"

Sarah glanced down to break eye contact with him. He knew that meant she was nervous about what his reaction might be to what she was about to say to him.

"I was just wondering…"

Sarah was looking down at her hands which were holding Michael's. Michael gave her a quizzical look.

"Yeah?"

She looked back up at him. She gazed deep into his eyes.

"What happened in there Michael? I mean between you and that...thing."

He could tell she was not comfortable saying the word, but he felt it needed to be said, not saying it did not change what it was.

"You mean the demon."

Sarah squeezed his had tightly, her voice was low and quiet, as if trying to talk about some terrible secret. She turned her gaze down to their hands again.

"Yeah."

Michael shook his head and spoke softly to her.

"Sarah. After all you saw and experienced that night, do you mean to tell me you're still not sure if you believe demons exist?"

Sarah kept her head down.

"I...I do I guess...I'm still just trying to make sense of it all. Michael that boy died. I'm not so sure it wasn't our fault, that we're not responsible..."

Michael's tone became more serious and he shifted to sit himself up. He squeezed her hand tightly.

"Okay, hold it right there. Whether you believe it was a demon or you believe that the boy was just mentally ill, he jumped from that balcony on his own. We did all we could to save the boy. All of us."

She could hear the firmness in his tone. She looked back into his eyes.

"I know, I just...when Jeff and I were heading back to the room. I could hear you talking to him, to the demon. I need to know what was said, what happened between you two? Why, if it was a demon, did it take the boy instead of you? The EVP we heard that night, before it all happened, it said it wanted your soul. So why didn't it take you instead of Jeremy?"

Michael looked into her eyes. He truly wished he had the answer to that himself.

"What was said between me and the demon doesn't matter."

Michael saw the look on Sarah's face begin to change to one of frustration.

"Wait, let me finish."

Sarah relaxed and waited for his answer.

"What matters is that it gave me its' name, and with that it gave me control over it."

Sarah's eyes lit up. She knew that was extremely important to the work they do and it was something she had not expected. Her interest was now peaked and she wanted to know what Michael knew.

"So what was the demons name?!"

Michael smiled and spoke softly.

"Come closer and I'll whisper it to you. Understand that you're never to say it out loud or tell it to anyone else. To say it out loud would mean to summon it, and this is a bad one Sarah, that's why you're not to tell anyone else either. Promise me."

Sarah understood and nodded her agreement.

"I promise Michael, I won't."

She leaned over and put her ear near his lips, and he whispered the name to her. She sat back up with a puzzled look on her face.

"So who is that?"

Michael smiled.

"That I'll leave for you to look up for yourself. You can find it in the Book of Enoch."

Sarah went back to her second question.

"So why didn't it take you Michael? Why Jeremy?"

Michael shook his head and looked straight into her eyes so she would know he was telling her the truth.

"I don't know Sarah. I truly don't know. God knows I wish it had taken me instead of the boy, but it didn't. The only thing I can piece together is that it felt it only had time to take one of us, it wanted both but only had time for one because of you and Jeff breaking down the door. It knew I had its name, it knew I could banish it if I came to. It already had control of Jeremy and it was out of time. Jeremy was the easy choice. The truth is though it has all the time in the universe to plot and plan its next move. They don't work on our time schedule you know. I'm sure it probably planned its next possession months or even years before it took control of Jeremy."

Sarah still did not understand the whole demonology, exorcism thing.

"Michael, if that's the case then how, how do we ever beat these things?"

He could see the look of distress on her face. Michael pulled her closer to him and gave her a long passionate kiss. Then he sat back and again looked deep into her beautiful green eyes. He spoke gently to her.

"Sarah, we don't beat them. Not really. We can only attempt to help save human souls from them. They are far too strong for us mortals to defeat. Only God himself and his angels can do that, and before you ask, the answer to why God doesn't do that is "free will". God gave us that, just as he gave it to his angels. They, like us, were free to choose right from wrong, the easy path from the hard one. These demons, these fallen angels, they don't give man that choice once they take possession, from that point on it is only the demons' will that rules your mind, not your own. All we can do is try to help those who are oppressed or possessed by these demons to find their way back to the light. To help them regain their free will. That's all we can do."

Sarah finally understood what Michael was trying to teach her, to get through to her. The choice was hers now whether she wanted to follow him on this path or to take a different one of her own, a safer one. It was time to exercise her own free will that God had given her. The truth though was that she had already made her choice that night at the Casey home. She loved Michael and would stand with him at the gates of hell itself if that's where their path took them. She squeezed his hands tight, then leaned into him and kissed him gently on the lips, then his cheek. She held her face against his. She squeezed him close. He could feel the tears streaming down her face as she whispered into his ear.

"Michael Gabriel Kenna, I love you with all my heart and all my soul and I will never, ever, leave your side."

"Have no fear of moving into the unknown. Simply step out fearlessly knowing that I am with you, therefore no harm can befall you; all is very, very well. Do this in complete faith and confidence."

~ Pope John Paul II ~

ABOUT S.P.I.R.I.T.S. OF NEW ENGLAND
http://www.spiritsofnewengland.org

As I discussed at the beginning of this book, S.P.I.R.I.T.S. of New England® was found in January of 2009 by Ellen MacNeil, Beck Gann and Sharon Koogler and is based in the city of Winthrop, Massachusetts just outside of Boston.

S.P.I.R.I.T.S. stands for Supernatural, Paranormal, Investigations, Research, Intuitive, Truth Society of New England and we exist to help those people and businesses who believe they are experiencing paranormal activity.

We travel within the New England States as well as NY, PA, and NJ. If you reside outside of these States we work in, please feel free to contact us for assistance and we will do our best to recommend a reliable and professional Paranormal Team to assist you.

We are a small group of dedicated Paranormal Investigators that will come to you and use scientific techniques to help find out what the activity is in your home. We conduct ourselves as professionals and take the work we do seriously. You can talk to us and we will listen, and do our best to make you comfortable in your own home again.

A lot of activity can be caused by plumbing issues, old homes as they age naturally, heating issues, etc. but when we cannot find a logical explanation, then we bring out the scientific equipment to identify the cause. Our group consists people that have had their own paranormal experiences to total skeptics but we all share a love for the Paranormal and the search of unanswered questions.

Please contact us through our website and let us help you. We do not charge any fee for helping you! Ever!

OUR INVESTIGATION SERVICES ARE ALWAYS FREE!

It is an honor for us to come to your home and the more investigations we do, the more we learn and can help others.

MEET THE S.P.I.R.I.T.S. TEAM

Ellen MacNeil

Founder, Lead Investigator, Case Manager. Ellen grew up being hopelessly addicted to horror movies, Dark Shadows, Hammer films from England with Christopher Lee and Peter Cushing, scary books and questioning "what's out there"? Now as an adult she is an avid fan of Ghost Hunters, Ghost Hunters International, Paranormal State and any other shows, documentaries and any books on the Paranormal she can find! She knew her brother had been killed in Vietnam the day it happened as the Army did not come to their door until the next day, "he sent very powerful messages to prepare us for this news", that opened up a whole new world to Ellen of the "unexplained". Ellen is very proud of her wonderful team of paranormal lovers including her partner Beck, and their daughter Sarah. She looks forward to all their upcoming investigations. During the day Ellen works at Brigham and Women's Hospital, dreaming of fried clams, The Rolling Stones, her cats and gardening. At night, give her a flashlight and off into the darkness she and her team go!

Beck Gann

Founder and Lead Investigator, Beck grew up in the southern state of Georgia. It was there that she had her first experience with the paranormal. The experience is something that Beck does not like to talk about as it was a very difficult time for her and her family. The experience did leave Beck a stronger person though and a person that is loving, caring and dedicated to her family and the ones she loves, especially Sarah and Ellen. Beck has a unique talent for being able to connect with clients who believe they are experiencing something paranormal and comforting them with the fact that they are not alone and not crazy, having experienced the paranormal first hand, Beck knows for a fact that the paranormal does exist, and that the fear that some people experience when confronted with it is very real as well.

Sharon Koogler

Co-Founder and Tech Department Manager. Having been raised on horror and sci-fi movies, Sharon has always had an interest in the supernatural/paranormal. She had some experiences as a child that she could not explain at the time. When she was older she was able to de-bunk some of those, but others.... It was a combination of movies and her own experiences that led her to the path of investigation to try to get some answers. Sharon is very proud of her team, especially the wonderful chemistry between them. She has been on numerous investigations, including Mt. Washington Hotel with members of T.A.P.S. in April '09 and boot camp at the Spalding Inn May 30th '09.

During the day Sharon works for two radiation oncologists at Brigham and Women's Hospital in Boston. At night she works as drum tech to four different drummers, and investigates as often as she can! She currently lives with her sister Hillary Blaze, drummer for Judas Priestess, The World's ONLY All Girl Tribute To The Metal Gods! Sharon misses both her French Bulldog, Aspect Jason Voorhees Trebor, and Malachi her Siberian Husky (15 years together).

Sharon, along with team member Jack Kenna, has appeared on numerous episodes of Haunted Case Files which is produced by Our House Media and airs on cable network Destination America.

Sarah Campbell

Investigator and Technical Assistant. Sarah is the daughter of S.P.I.R.I.T.S. Founders Ellen and Beck. Her interest in the paranormal began at a very young age when she had her own experience. Sarah, like her mom and Beck, is very dedicated to her family, including her extended family in the S.P.I.R.I.T.S. team. She studied graphic design in college, she also helps to create various designs for her mother's business Madcatter Design. Sarah also works as a medical assistant at Brigham and Women's Hospital in Boston with her mother and Sharon. She also has a passion for fictional writing, sailing, and website design. She is a major Doctor Who fan and admires the character Missy, AKA The Master, the Doctors arch enemy. When attending Comic Cons, you can typically find Sarah cosplaying as Missy, so keep an eye out for her.

Jack Kenna

Investigator, Technical Specialist, Writer, New York State Chapter of S.P.I.R.I.T.S. of New England. Jack is also a member of two other paranormal teams; San Diego Ghost Hunters in San Diego, CA founded by Maritza Skandunas, and Extreme Paranormal Encounter Response Team (ExPERT) based in Cohoes, NY and founded by Stacey Horton. Jack is also an honorary member of Wraith Paranormal Research Society (WPRS) located in North Carolina, founded by Wendy Young and Eric Haas and mentored by Jack.

Born in Troy, NY in January 1963, Jack grew up in an area rich in history, legends, haunted graveyards, historical buildings, and Revolutionary War Battlefields. Jack's interest in the paranormal started at a very young age. This was driven by the fact that his mother had many experiences of her own which she often relayed to him. The home he grew up in and now raises his family in also helped to peak his interest in the paranormal, in addition to his wife and their seven children it is also home to what he refers to as a friendly spirit, which seems to keep an eye out for the family. In more recent years his interest in the paranormal was rekindled by the TV series Ghost Hunters and the scientific investigation methods utilized by TAPS. These methods are very similar to the type of engineering and scientific methods that Jack has been using on a daily basis for the past thirty plus years in his career as a Senior Engineering Technician and project leader for the Department of the Army. Beyond his technical expertise for the Army, Jack brings to the S.P.I.R.I.T.S. team his video and audio skills from six years of running his own part-time videography business, as well as his computer and website design skills from seven years of running his own part-time computer repair, training, and web design business. Since 2011 Jack has also been writing paranormal articles and stories for Paranormal Underground and Living Paranormal Magazines as a regular contributor to both. Jack has another book being published in the spring of 2018 by Schiffer Publishing, Ltd.. This new book will be about investigating the paranormal, team building, and basic equipment and its practical uses for paranormal research. In 2015 Jack, along with illustrator Alex Cormack, completed work on the first issue of a new comic book series based on the teams' investigations, this first book is titled S.P.I.R.I.T.S. - The Forgotten Souls of Bay Path. Jack has also appeared in numerous episodes of the television series Paranormal Survivor (Seasons 1 & 2) as one of their paranormal experts. In 2016 he also appeared as a series lead in numerous episodes of the paranormal series titled Haunted Case Files. Both of these shows are produced by Our House Media (OHM) located in Toronto, Canada, and are aired in the U.S. on cable network Destination America. In 2017 Jack has continued working and consulting with OHM on Paranormal Survivor, Season 3 and another new series currently titled Scariest Night of My Life.

OTHER PROJECTS

I truly hope you enjoyed the stories within this book and found them at least entertaining. I know for my own part it was a pleasure and true enjoyment to write them. If you did enjoy this book you may also enjoy another work of mine, which I partnered with my friend Mr. Alex Cormack on to illustrate for me. It is the first in a series of comics entitled S.P.I.R.I.T.S. – The Forgotten Souls of Bay Path, and yes it is also based on one of the stories in this book, although if you liked that short story you may want to see how Alex brought it to life in comic form and how the story had to evolve in order to enter a visual medium. I think you might find it even more interesting. I have included a few of the pages here from the comic for your review and enjoyment. To purchase your own hard copy or digital copy of S.P.I.R.I.T.S. – The Forgotten Souls of Bay Path go to: http://www.indyplanet.us/product/131690/

Left to Right – Alex Cormack, Jack Kenna, and Missy; AKA – Sarah Campbell. Yes, once in a while we can even convince Missy to help promote S.P.I.R.I.T.S. although we do worry that one day she might turn us all into one.

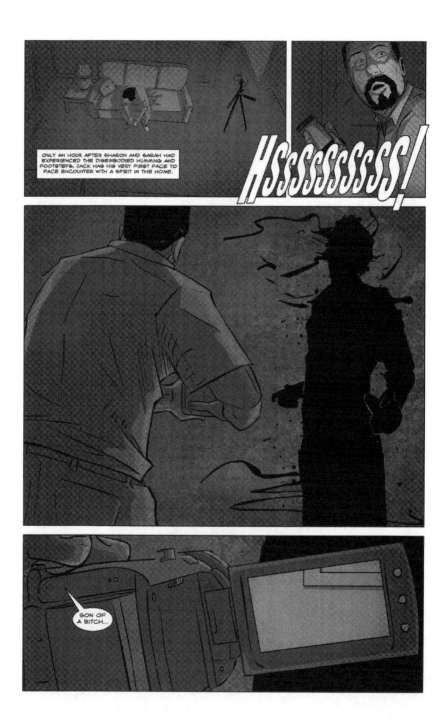

**S.P.I.R.I.T.S. – The Forgotten Souls of Bay Path
Available online in hard copy or digital copy from**

http://www.indyplanet.us/product/131690/

ALEX CORMACK

COMICS ILLUSTRATIONS ANIMATION SHOP CONTACT

Born October 8, 1982, is an American comic book illustrator. He has
best known for his work on the "Oxymoron" series from
ComixTribe and "I Play the Bad Guy" from Bliss on Tap Publishing.
- From Wikipedia, the free encyclopedia –
Alex is also the illustrator for:
S.P.I.R.I.T.S. - The Forgotten Souls of Bay Path
Find out more about Alex and his work at his website
http://alexcormack.com/

CURRENT TELEVISION PROJECTS

Produced by Our House Media
and airs in Canada, the USA, the U.K., and Germany

Also airs in the U.K. and Europe as

Produced by Our House Media and
airs in Canada, the USA, the U.K., and Germany
All shows air in the USA on cable network Destination America, check
with your local cable provider for channels and listings.

CONTACT THE AUTHOR

Whether you have a paranormal related question, need help with a possible haunting, or would like to have Jack speak or lecture at your event, you can reach out to him through the following media options:

1. S.P.I.R.I.T.S. of New England website at:
    http://www.spiritsofnewengland.org

2. Facebook: https://www.facebook.com/JackNY45

3. Email: jack.kenna.paranormal@gmail.com

"I don't care what you believe in, just believe in it."

Shepard Book – Serenity (2005)

RAMBLINGS

THE DARK SIDE OF THE PARANORMAL

Almost every investigator in the paranormal field today, including myself, has been drawn to it because they either had their own personal experience, wanted to have their own experience, were motivated by their love of the unexplained, by investigators they had seen on TV or met in person, or by the Hollywood movies that they had seen as kids. Most, if not all of us, came into this field with the same good intentions; to help further the field of paranormal studies and to try and help others who were experiencing things that they just could not find a rational explanation for, things that chilled and frightened them to their core, things that could not and cannot be totally explained even today by the accepted modern sciences.

We paranormal investigators have been and continue to be a very unique, unconventional and extremely diverse group of people. We come from all walks of life, all backgrounds, all education levels, all ethnicities, and all parts of the world. It is our diversity that makes us strong, and it is that same diversity that can, at times, tear us apart. It has been and always will be a two edged sword, as with diversity comes divergent and often clashing ideas, methodologies, opinions, and viewpoints.

Now none of what I have just mentioned is a bad thing, at least not in and of itself. The true pitfalls here in the paranormal community are not the ideas, not the opinions or viewpoints we all have, but how each of us treats those that do not agree with us. How we react when someone offers a counter opinion or viewpoint to our own, or how we talk negatively about someone because of the success they are having, or their lack of success for that matter. This is where we often do the most harm, not only to each other but to this field of study which we are a part of. We can be a very jealous, envious and hurtful lot when we choose to be, and trust me it is not a pretty sight. Within our community it is referred to as para-drama, and in many cases can be as bad as what you see or read about high school kids doing to each other these days, and these are adults I'm discussing here.

Don't get me wrong, we are not the only group of people out there that act this way. I have worked in the engineering and scientific community for over thirty years, and I have seen this same behavior in this field of work as well. The big difference, and in my opinion "problem", is that unlike some of these other more "established" fields of scientific study and professionals, we tend to wear our hearts on our sleeves so to speak. We post our outrages and our hurtful, and harmful, statements and opinions on Facebook, Twitter, and every other means of social media out on the internet that we can find, for everyone in the world to see. Instantly posting our unfounded and/or un-thought out opinions, which are usually based in anger or jealousy, as statements of fact. We do this without thought given to the consequences of our actions, not just to those that we have something against, but also without thought to the consequences to ourselves and the Paranormal Community as a whole. Any of us who have spent any amount of time in this field have seen what I'm talking about here. We have seen the reputations, and in some cases careers, of individuals in our field ruined within a day because of an unfounded and unsubstantiated rumor that someone has posted about them, and some of us are just as quick to jump on the band wagon with a gang mentality to help spread the rumors, taking what was said as the truth without even discussing it or questioning the source from which it came.

This is not the only problem currently plaguing our Paranormal Community though. There is something even darker and more harmful to all of us lurking out there, that we all have been seeing occur more and more in recent years. The "manufacturing" of evidence by unscrupulous so called "investigators" is nothing new mind you. It has gone on in this field of study since it was first founded, and it occurs for the same reasons now as it did in the beginning, to feed ego and to try and capture fame and fortune. What did you say? You do not believe that anyone is in this field would do this just to gain fame and fortune? Think again. True, there are a few, a very few, in the Paranormal Community that have gained some type of fame and success from their work. We all know who these individuals are, and in my own opinion they have earned their success through their hard work and years of dedication to this field of study. These people have done more than their share to advance the Paranormal Sciences into becoming a much more accepted scientific field by the general public. They did not and do not "seek" fame and success, that was never their intention, but through their hard work, dedication and perhaps a little luck, it found them. I'm not just talking about the people you see on TV either. I'm talking about many others whose numerous books, lectures and years of hard work and sacrifice have made them icons in our field of work. There are those though who have tried to take a short cut. They have tried to turn this field into their own private "cash cow", by creating evidence and trying to pass it off as real evidence of the paranormal. They do this just like the old fake fortune tellers did. They create false photos, videos, EVPs and other false evidence during investigations, especially during their so called "haunted tours" or on their internet videos in order to try and impress their followers, clients and other investigators who work in this field of study. "So what" you may say. Who cares what a handful of untrustworthy people may be doing. The answer is simple, we should all care because we are all affected by what they do! Here again, through the internet and social networks they instantly distribute their creations to the world, not giving any thought to the inevitable negative impact to our Paranormal Community and to the credibility of our field of work. Every time a new fraud is exposed, the hardcore skeptics and those who hate, yes hate, the Paranormal Community use it as an opportunity to stand on their soap box and shout to the world how this proves that we are ALL frauds and the paranormal is nothing but a sham!

So what should and what can we do about it? I personally believe that we need to start by each of us doing more oversight of ourselves and the teams that we belong to. We need to create ourselves into a true organization of professionals, with codes of conduct and a standard of ethics. We need to stop being jealous of the success of others and start working together to advance this field of work into one that is respected and accepted as a legitimate science. I know, it's all just a pipe dream and wishful thinking you say. Perhaps, but did not all great discoveries and great advancements in history just start off as someone's dream?

The above article first appeared in Paranormal Underground Magazine in April 2011.

BEGININGS

When my friends Alex and Helena King of Boleyn Paranormal in the UK asked me if I would write an article for the first issue of their new magazine Living Paranormal, I was more than happy to oblige, and very honored that they asked me. When we discussed what they would like me to write about, they asked if I could write about one of my investigations that had not yet been aired on the television shows, or that I had already written about in my upcoming book. As I have also just begun working on another book and have some additional stories in the works for my comic book series, this made me think for a bit about what I could share that you might find interesting while also being unique, and not part of any projects I am working on. What I have decided to share with you is my very first, and I mean very first, real investigation of reported spirit activity in the home where my mother grew up in Troy, New York.

Just to give you a little background, my mother's home in Troy was a small two story house, where her family had lived for over fifty years. Her sister and brother, both of whom never married, lived in the house until their deaths. My cousin then lived in it for several more years after purchasing it from the family. At least four family members died in the home, including my grandfather and grandmother and my aunt and uncle. The family also used to talk about the ghosts that lived in the house shortly after they first moved in back in the late 1930's. My mother specifically talked about a spirit on the second floor, in their parent's bedroom, that insisted on the walk-in closet door being left open. It was after my aunts' death in the home in the mid 1980's, long before television shows like Ghost Hunters ever came along, that I would have the unexpected opportunity to actually check out this reported haunting in the family home. Here is how it all came about....

A few weeks after my aunts' funeral my mother, being the sole surviving immediate family member, had to go to the old house to meet with one of her nieces to go over what was left in the estate and discuss the pending sale of the home. I drove her to the house and was there for moral support.

Now this was a house that I had visited many, many times over the years and so I knew it well, having spent many a Thanksgiving and Christmas day in the home. For the most part, as a child and young teenager I never really noticed anything odd about the house, until I would go upstairs to the bathroom. The upstairs always had a completely different feel to it, just a feeling like someone was always watching you. Now in those early days I never really thought too much about ghost or hauntings so I just never made much of it, just did what I had to do and got the heck back down stairs. By the time of my aunts death though, I was now in my early 20's and had a real interest in the paranormal, always watching shows like "In Search Of" hosted by Leonard Nimoy, reading books like "The Amityville Horror", and watching movies like "The Exorcist" all very cool stuff, but what I found more intriguing were the stories my mother shared with me about her own paranormal experiences, one of which was what I described early to you about the door in the upstairs bedroom never staying closed.

Now understand that in the 1980's we did not have things like smart phones or iPhones and I did not have any recording equipment with me or a camera or any equipment at all. What I had with me in the house was "me". After spending about an hour down stairs in the house with my mother and my cousin, I needed to head upstairs to use the bathroom. The stairway to the second floor is actually in the front of the house, so I had to walk through the dining room and living room to get to the stairway. Reaching the top of stairs on the second floor you enter into a hallway with a room to the left and one to the right, then the bathroom also on the right and at the end of the hallway is a door that enters into the master bedroom. As you go into that room you also have to step down three short stairs, the room is about 3.5 meters (11 ft.) square. On the right was the door to the walk-in closet which is actually almost another small room which is about 1.5 meters (5 ft.) x 3.5 meters (11 ft.). The moment that I reached the top of the stairs and the entrance to the hallway, that the feeling of being watched came over me, and sent a bit of a chill through me. It was at that moment that I remembered the story my mother told me about the door, and so I decided to check it out and see if there was really anything to it. It was getting later in the evening and the sun was just beginning to set, there were no lights on upstairs so what light there was, was from the setting sun shining through the windows, which made it all a bit eerie from the shadows that were being cast throughout the hall and the rooms.

I decided to forego the bathroom break for the moment and see if there really was anything to this "ghost" wanting the closet door kept open. I walked down the hallway and stood at the entrance to the master bedroom. I paused for a moment. That uncomfortable feeling of being watched seemed to be even stronger at this end of the hallway, or was it really just the fact that I knew I was alone upstairs and the stories of ghosts was getting to me. Remember again that at this point in the mid 1980's the only thing most of us knew about ghosts was from what we knew from movies and television, which like today only portrayed them as evil or demonic things that could hurt you or would try to possess you and take your soul. Perhaps because of this, young people like me, who had a curious interest in the paranormal were a bit more naïve about movies and television and we believed what they showed us. There were no Ghost Hunters or Paranormal shows to give us a glimpse of what paranormal investigating was really like, and talking about it was taboo in those days. If you really believed in ghosts you were either insane, weird or involved in devil worship and the occult. Also, social media was the local newspaper, there was no Facebook, Twitter, or Blogs where you could go to easily find like-minded people to discuss these things with; you were basically on your own, which is exactly what I was standing at the threshold to the room. Little did I know I was also literally standing at the threshold to my involvement in the true realm of the paranormal investigating, this was the moment that my journey into the paranormal truly began.

As I stared into the room from the doorway, something I was sensing made me feel that I should perhaps announce myself to whatever might be in the room before entering it. Since the door to the room was already open, I knocked twice on the doorframe, "Hello, this is Jack, Helen's son. Do you mind if I come in?" Yes, I actually asked if it was okay to enter the room, I think I actually half expected an answer as well, or at least some sign, but there was nothing but silence. The room was completely still. In hind sight I believe that was an answer of sorts, at least as best any spirit might be able to answer. Nothing happened. Nothing was thrown at me. No disembodied voice or growl telling me to "Get out!" No foul smells. I guess even today I would take that as a "Yes, sure, come on in." I waited for a moment and then walked down the three steps into the room. Nothing, no reaction from anything. I looked at the door to the closet and noticed that it was open about one third of a meter. I walked toward the closet and as I did I spoke again to whatever spirit might be there. "My mother told me that you don't like this door to be closed, is that true?" I now stood in front of the closet door. Still that feeling of being watched was nagging at me. I reached out for the door knob. "I'm not trying to be rude or anything, but I just want to know if you are really here or not. I'm going to close this door, and if you are here, can you please re-open it for me?" I pulled the door shut and let go to see if it remained latched. It did. I grabbed the door knob again and pushed and pulled on it to be sure it would not just pop open. It was solidly latched. I let go and it remained shut. I took three steps back from the door. "Can you open the door for me please?" I stood and just watched, hoping that the door would open. Nothing. It remained shut. I asked again, "Can you please open the door? I just want to know if you are here." I stood and watched for at least a full minute. Nothing. It was at this point that I felt the need to finally relieve myself, which is what I had originally headed up to the second floor for. Disappointed, I headed off out of the room to the bathroom. A few moments later I came back out of the bathroom and because of its location to the master bedroom, when I came out I was able to glance down towards the bedroom and see the closet door. The door was open. It did surprise me; I really was not expecting to see that door open. I knew it was firmly shut, but there it was, open as wide as it had first been. I walked back down in the room and to the closet door. I closely inspected the door and the latch, nothing seemed wrong or out of place. "Did you open the door?" I asked. No response, nor did I really expect one. My first thought was not that it was a ghost that opened it, but that maybe when I walked away I put some kind of pressure on the floor that made the door latch spring open, and I just had not heard it or noticed it. I pulled the door shut again, checking to make sure it was tightly latched and then I began rocking my feet on the floor, stepping back several feet and walking between the door and the stairs to try and get the door to open. Again, nothing happened, the door remained shut.

At this point I was a perplexed as to how the door had opened when I know it was firmly shut. I asked again for any spirit that might be there to open the door for me please. Again I stood and watched for several minutes. The door remained shut. I decided that my experiment was over, there was no ghost, it was just all coincidence, something with the doorframe or the floor boards that I that could not replicate. It was all just random. I turned, my back now to the door, and began to walk up the three steps to the hallway.... "CLICK!" The sound was loud and obvious. I hesitated for just a moment before turning back to look at the door, it was half way open and I could easily see into the closet. I wanted to walk back to the door, but I found myself frozen, just for a moment, as a wave of chills ran up through my whole body. I did not realize this at the time, but as I later did more and more investigations, and to this day, this is a sign for me that a spirit is present in a location and is trying to communicate.

I composed myself and slowly walked back to the door. "Hello?" I think I mostly said this just to make myself feel better, to at least hear the sound of a human voice even if it was my own. I approached the door, grabbed the door knob and opened the door the rest of the way. No one was there, the closet was empty, but there did seem to be a heaviness to the small room. I still was not totally ready to believe this was the work of a ghost, it must have something to do with the door latch popping open when I stepped onto the three steps leading up to the hallway, I had not tried that during my first debunking effort, so I would try it again this time. I closed the door again, and once again made sure it was securely shut and latched. This time I decided to walk backwards away from the door, so I could see when it opened and know where on the floor or steps was causing the latch to spring. I stepped firmly but slowly backwards, moving away from the door, glancing back quickly just to check my distance from the stairs. Once I reached the stairs I walked up them backwards, watching the door as I did so. I reached the top of the stairs and watched from the doorway to the room. The closet door remained closed. I walked up and down the three steps several times, the closet door remained shut. I decided to walk backwards down the hallway, about half way, so that I could still see the closet door. Still the closet door remained shut. I stood there quietly in the hallway, puzzling over what could have caused the door to open if not something in the floorboards or in the latch mechanism itself. I stood watching the door, waiting for it to open, because if it opened while I was watching it I might be able to figure out what was causing it. I stood there for what seemed like forever. Nothing. I gave a deep sigh. I decided that I better get back down stairs to my mom and her niece. I turned to go, no longer looking at the door…. "CLICK….CREEK." I FROZE IN PLACE! That wave of chills ran right up through me again, but this time I spun around quickly hoping to at least catch the door moving! Too late, the door was wide open this time!

What happened next I really did not expect of myself. Now you might think I would have run like hell out of there, so would I to be honest, but I did not. Strangely enough I found myself smiling, I actually chuckled. "Okay, I get it. You're here and you want that door open. I won't close it again I promise. Thank you for letting me know you really are here." I turned with a smile still on my face and walked back downstairs. This was first ever true investigation. No I did not have an audio recorder or a video camera, but I think if I had I would have at least captured one good EVP of perhaps one of my deceased relatives, or maybe the original owner thanking me for acknowledging them, and maybe I would have caught the door actually opening on camera, but the truth is that does not really matter. What matters is what I felt during that experience and the feeling of comfort and satisfaction I had when I walked away. I do believe to this day this is why I look at hauntings in a slightly different way than many investigators. I do not consider all hauntings demonic or evil, I think that many hauntings are just misunderstood, and it is often out of frustration or angst that spirits sometimes cause problems or even physical damage to those they are haunting. Not that there are not true demonic or evil spirits, there are, but maybe we need to consider some other possibilities before jumping to that conclusion. This is just my personal opinion.

We all started our journey into the real paranormal somewhere, this was mine beginning, it has lead me in a direction that I had never imagined I would go in my life, as I am sure it has for all of you. The path you take on this unique journey is up to. My advice is not to follow the herd. Follow your own path and be true to your own beliefs about the paranormal, but always keep an open mind and listen and learn from others as well.

The above article first appeared in Living Paranormal Magazine in February 2017.

SPIRIT ATTACHMENT, SPIRIT POSSESSION, OR PARANORMAL REFUGEE?

Anyone who knows me knows I am not a very political person, but the protests, debates and court actions regarding the temporary ban on refugees from seven middle eastern countries, and how various groups, political parties and individuals view refugees and the rights that should be afforded them got me thinking about how we in the paranormal community view what we call spirit attachments and possessions. We all see these things as purely negative and harmful to the individual being affected. We concern ourselves with helping the person experiencing the attachment or the possession with no thought given to the spirit who has attached themselves or taken possession of the human, but what about them? What happens to the spirit when we remove or banish them? Should we not also be concerned for the attached or possessing entity at least as much as we are for the human they are attached to or possessing? I know what you're thinking: "What are you talking about?! Have you lost your mind?!" Maybe I have, but all I ask is that you hear me out before you decide to banish me instead of the entities.

Let us start with something we can mostly all agree upon, that attachments and/or possessions typically occur to a living person that either knowingly or unwittingly has invited the opportunity for an entity to attach to or possess them. We have seen this time and time again with people who watch the TV shows going out on their own to investigate a haunted location, like they see the people on television do, but with no knowledge of real paranormal investigating or how to protect themselves from the spirit world. They go out looking to have an "experience", to see a ghost, to have fun, etc. Then there are those that delve into the dark arts, satanic rituals, or decide to use a spirit board in their own home to invite an entity to come to them. Yes, most of these people have no clue what they are really doing or asking for, but is that the fault of the entity that they have conjured up or openly invited into their life? This is where I think a better term for these entities that have been invited by the human to cross the spiritual border into their life would be "Paranormal Refugee". If we consider that many of us in the paranormal community believe that there are spirits and entities out there that are lost, confused, frightened, and also just plain evil that are looking for an opportunity to get out of their current private hell of being trapped in a location or spiritual limbo, can we truly be angry or upset with them, or even want to banish them back to the terrible place they came from, when they have been freely invited by a living human being to be given refuge from their plight by that persons intentional, albeit often naive, actions?

So here in lies my concern of such situations. For whom should we seasoned investigators of the paranormal be more sympathetic towards; The displaced, forgotten, abandoned entity that was openly and freely invited into the life of the living human, or for the person who thought it would be *fun* to go *ghost hunting* and have an *experience*, or who decided to dabble in dark magic or satanic worship, or the person who thought it would be *fun* or *cool* to try and conjure a spirit through a spirit board to see what would happen, and in doing so opened the spiritual border for an entity to cross over and become part of that person's life.

So again I ask, might not these Paranormal Refugees deserve at least as much of our sympathy as the people affected by these entities that we are called upon to help? Do not at least some of these entities deserve our help as well? I believe it is at least something to consider, then again, maybe this whole commentary is nothing more than just satirical sarcasm based on current events, but that is for you to decide.

~Jack Kenna

SITTING IN DARKNESS
A Poem By Jack Kenna

Sitting in darkness
In an abandoned building
Speaking to the darkness
To something I cannot see
To something that may or may not exist
Hoping that it does
Hoping that it hears me
Hoping for it to answer
Listening for a response
For a sound
A noise
Anything
Please
Hear me
Answer me
I need to know
I am not alone
I am not insane
That there is more after this life
That the essence of who we are lives on
Please
Answer me

The above poem was first published in Living Paranormal Magazine
in April 2017.

A FINAL WORD

The stories you just read would seem to be works of pure fiction simply pulled from the mind of the author, but the fact is that a good number of the experiences described in these stories are pulled from actual events, experiences, and evidence captured by the *S.P.I.R.I.T.S. of New England* team during several of their investigations. Again, not all of these stories are based on actual events, but much of the activity described in them is based on documented experiences of real paranormal activity. Shadow figures, objects moving, strange light anomalies, hearing dis-embodied voices, being scratched and/or grabbed by something that cannot been seen, demonic possession it all does exist and is real, I have seen much of it firsthand.

I realize there will always be skeptics or those who just do not, and will not believe in such things, and that is fine. I do not seek to change anyone's mind about what they believe to be real or the truth. What I do hope for is to open up peoples' minds to the possibilities that there is more to the world than meets the eye, or than what can be proven by science alone. I hope to, if nothing else, entertain you with stories that seem far beyond belief. For those who may read this book that work in the paranormal as me and my team do, I hope some of the stories make you smile, laugh, and even bring a chill to you as you find something familiar in them that reminds you of your own investigations and experiences.

The investigations and experiences of S.P.I.R.I.T.S. of New England or of Michael, Sarah and the RePR team do not end here with this book. They still go on in the investigations and experiences of all paranormal teams and all those experiencing paranormal activity that need our help. To be a part of a paranormal team is something special, something to not be taken lightly, something that requires dedication and passion in order to help those who have nowhere else to turn to for answers. It is like no other field of study out there, as there is no money to be made in true paranormal investigating and research. While you can, and some have, made a career in this field, the work they have done has not paid their bills, they have a full-time job for that.

What we do, we do to help others, to find answers, and to move the field of paranormal research forward inch by inch in the hopes we may someday understand what lies beyond the veil, what happens to who we are after our bodies have failed us. This book did not and does not pretend to attempt to answer those questions, but it does attempt to make you think and to entertain you. I hope it has accomplished both of those things for you. ~ Jack Kenna

"I believe in everything until it's disproved. So I believe in fairies, the myths, dragons. It all exists, even if it's in your mind. Who's to say that dreams and nightmares aren't as real as the here and now?"

~ John Lennon ~

Made in the USA
Middletown, DE
17 January 2020